THE BORROWED HOUSE

By Hilda van Stockum

A Day on Skates
The Cottage at Bantry Bay
Francie on the Run
Kersti and St. Nicholas
Pegeen
Andries
Gerrit and the Organ
The Mitchells
Canadian Summer
The Angels' Alphabet
Patsy and the Pup
King Oberon's Forest
Friendly Gables
Little Old Bear
The Winged Watchman
Jeremy Bear
Bennie and the New Baby
New Baby is Lost
Mogo's Flute
Penengro
Rufus Round and Round
The Borrowed House

The Borrowed House

Hilda van Stockum

Purple House Press
Kentucky

Published by
Purple House Press
PO Box 787, Cynthiana, Kentucky 41031

Classic Living Books for Kids and Young Adults
purplehousepress.com

Text and cover illustration copyright © 1975 by Hilda van Stockum.
Cover illustration and author self-portrait used with permission from
the estate of Hilda van Stockum and Boissevain Books.

Library of Congress Cataloging-in-Publication Data

Names: Van Stockum, Hilda, 1908-2006, author.
Title: The borrowed house / by Hilda van Stockum.
Description: Kentucky : Purple House Press, [2016] | Summary: "During
  World War II a young German girl, member of the Hitler Youth, goes to
  live with her parents in occupied Amsterdam and comes to realize the
  truth about the war while living in a house requisitioned for her family"
  —Provided by publisher.
Identifiers: LCCN 2016021523 | ISBN 9798888018009 (pbk. : alk. paper)
Subjects: LCSH: World War, 1939-1945—Netherlands—Juvenile fiction. |
  CYAC: World War, 1939-1945—Netherlands—Fiction. |
  Netherlands—History—German occupation, 1940-1945—Fiction.
Classification: LCC PZ7.V36 Bo 2016 | DDC [Fic]—dc23
LC record available at https://lccn.loc.gov/2016021523

To my twin cousin, Nella,
in memory of happy childhood days.

Contents

	Foreword	9
1	The Ring of Power	13
2	Crossing the Rhine	26
3	The Arrival	38
4	The House	46
5	A Fountain in the Garden	61
6	The Play	69
7	A Tea Party	77
8	The Birthday	91
9	Lessons	107
10	Sef	117
11	The Accident	126
12	Janna Helps Out	137
13	Troubles	144
14	Betrayal	153
15	Hugo	161
16	The Lost Siegfried	166
17	The Picture	171
18	The Ball	186
19	Twilight of the Gods	196
	Afterword	205

"Self-Portrait" by Hilda van Stockum (1968).
Painted in the technique used by Dutch Masters and early Renaissance painters.

Foreword

This book, *The Borrowed House*, is about Hitler's occupation of Holland in 1940-1945, from the perspective of a German girl, Janna Oster. She travels from the Black Forest in Germany to her parents in Amsterdam. When we first meet her, Janna is memorizing Hitler's theories of racial supremacy for a school test. How could she know, or even imagine, the ultimate implications of these theories, fulfilled in death camps like Auschwitz and Treblinka?

Later, when Janna discovers that someone she actually cares about is from one of the races she was taught were "inferior," it comes as a shock to her. She is angry that the theories she was carefully taught conflict with her warm feelings for a real human being. Can she reconcile her feelings with the theories?

Those who resisted Hitler paid the ultimate price. Many people in World War II were reluctant heroes, acting against a monstrous evil. When the Dutch Royal Family, in exile, called Dutch Resistance leaders heroes, they objected. "We only did our duty," they said. "Can you say No, when you are the only person who can prevent someone's death?"

Today, we often complacently believe our country would never succumb to a demagogue like Hitler. In the wake of the 9/11 attacks we saw widespread signs in America of selflessness, of men and women in uniform rushing to save innocent people, and our hearts were with them. But the same uniting behind the victims of 9/11 also generated a wish for revenge and exacerbated fears of people with certain religious beliefs or appearance. If a time comes when we again have to make difficult choices, how thoughtful and brave will we be?

As a young boy growing up in Washington, D.C. and then Montreal, I heard a lot about bravery and moral choices made at great personal cost. My mother, Hilda van Stockum, talked for hours with her mother about the wartime suffering and courageous acts of their Dutch relatives. They spoke in Dutch, but I heard and understood the pain in their voices.

They had reason to lament. Dozens of my mother's Dutch cousins died, some are buried in *Erebegraafplaats*, the Dutch Cemetery of Heroes. More are honored with Yad Vashem awards for sheltering Jewish people. My mother's closest relative, her brother Willem, was an RAF bomber pilot; he was shot down in June 1944 and he is buried in Laval, France.

Through wartime letters, my mother was frequently in touch with her Dutch cousins. *The Borrowed House* is dedicated to one of them, her "twin cousin" Nella de Beaufort. Nella's younger brother Hans de Beaufort was a Resistance hero. He wrote a moving letter from prison in Dijon before he was killed by the Nazis. The closing lines (translated by my mother) were: "I did what I thought my duty. I did what I could but at a certain moment it is too much and you can't manage any more. From that moment you have to leave it all to God's care. Now I can happily say: 'Thy will be done' and give body and soul back to Him from Whom I got them."

For two decades, the losses were too painful for my mother to write about. But nearly 20 years after the end of the war, she wrote the first of her two books about the Dutch occupation, *The Winged Watchman*, which tells the story of how a rural family living in a windmill fought against Hitler and his followers. It was, like this book, fictionalized, but is based on her deep knowledge of Holland and the war, and wartime and postwar letters to her, and postwar visits with her relatives.

In 1975 she wrote this sequel based on a true story, *The Borrowed House*, about a German girl uprooted from her Hitler Youth program to live with her parents in an Amsterdam house that is "borrowed" from a Dutch family. It follows Janna from her first introduction to Amsterdam, where her parents were entertaining German troops, to her questioning of Hitler's theories of racial superiority.

Both of her books lead the reader to ask: "Would today's generation show such courage or be willing to make sacrifices of the kind that people made in World War II?" Many people say no, but we don't know what people are made of until they are faced with a crisis. B. Kelly, a graduate in English Literature from Bard College, has thoughtfully noted two compelling features about this book:

First, this book offers views of the Dutch occupation from the contrasting perspectives of the occupying Germans and the occupied Dutch. We meet many kinds of German and Dutch people, ranging from committed Nazis to people who are politically ambivalent. We glimpse the owners of the house, the van Arkels, through their home, art works and other possessions. We see how a transplanted German family adjusts to the sheltered life on Amsterdam's Emperor's Canal under the patronage of a German Baron and General.

Second, Hilda van Stockum shows how Janna is startled by her experiences, such as the contradiction between the propaganda she has been taught and the reality she sees. This gradually rising moral awareness may well be uncomfortable for us as readers, because it forces us to ask: "Would we have accepted Hitler's racial dogma just the way Janna does, when other children and people in authority were aligned with these theories?"

Hitler's propagandists were extremely good at what they did for their evil purpose. They linked Nazi views to ancient German and Greek myths through monument-building, music, children's camps and theater. Hilda van Stockum shows us through Janna just how effective this can be.

If we are sure that we would have been a hero like Hans de Beaufort in wartime, we should look closely at ourselves in the reflection from the windows of the van Arkel house. How immune are we really from racist and other ideology that continues to be sold and bought in a world where propaganda is a big business?

Hilda van Stockum's granddaughter Christine has written a brilliant analysis of the place of this book among van Stockum's writings. It appears at the end of this book. I am grateful to Jill Morgan and Purple House Press for re-issuing *The Borrowed House*.

John Tepper Marlin, July 2016

The Ring of Power

THE BARN SMELLED OF STALE HAY, chicken droppings, and cabbage. Lorelei, the white hen, cackled. With a swift glance over her shoulder, Janna took the broom and chased the bird off her nest. Sure enough, there was an egg. Janna slid it into her apron pocket. The barn door creaked as Frau Kopp came in, towering over Janna, a mountain of authority.

"Kill me a couple of chickens, Janna, quick," she said. "I've unexpected company." Janna looked around in dismay. What she saw were not chickens but Lorelei and Ilsebill, the leghorns; Wilhelm, the rooster; Fritz and Franz, the cockerels; Lieschen, Gretchen, and all the other cackling, scratching friends she knew by name. How could you kill something that had a name? But what could you do against a grownup? Janna began to sweep vigorously.

"Johanna," repeated Frau Kopp, "did you hear me?"

Janna looked up, shaking the hair out of her eyes. "I can't," she said, trembling at her own audacity.

"You *can*," Frau Kopp insisted. "I showed you. You wring their necks, like that...it's easy. What a fool they have sent me—and the other one so good, so willing! Why did she have to leave?"

"I'm on duty," said Janna desperately. "We have a Youth meeting."

"But it isn't Wednesday," protested Frau Kopp. "I know on Wednesdays you have your *Heimabend* and have to leave early. But today is Tuesday and you can help in the kitchen, can't you?"

"It's a special meeting," said Janna, noticing the frustrated expression on Frau Kopp's face. No one was allowed to interfere with the Hitler Youth meetings: not the church, or the school, parents or employers.

"A special meeting, a special meeting," grumbled Frau Kopp. "You are always having these special meetings and I think it's just to escape work. What's this meeting for, then?"

Janna's face lit up. "It's a rehearsal," she said. "We're going to do a play our group leader has written. And *imagine*...they've chosen *me* to be Brunhilde!"

"And who is Brunhilde?" asked Frau Kopp sourly.

"Don't you know? She is Siegfried's bride. He gives her the magic ring, which was stolen from the Rhine maidens. But there is a curse on it. Siegfried drinks an evil potion, forgets Brunhilde, and marries someone else. Brunhilde is furious and causes him to die, but she is sorry afterward, and when she lights his funeral pyre she jumps on it herself, and as they burn all the gods burn with them."

Frau Kopp had listened open-mouthed. "Where do you get all that heathenish nonsense?"

"Oh, it isn't nonsense," said Janna. "It's all in Wagner's operas."

"It's heathenish anyway," sputtered Frau Kopp. "And for that they keep you from honest work!"

"Learning a part is work too. My parents have to do it all the time. They're famous actors, their pictures are often in the papers, and Hitler has praised them. It's in an article...I'll show it to you....He says they are an outstanding example of true Aryan culture."

"I know, I know," Frau Kopp interrupted, "you've told me before. Isn't it early for you to go? Your meetings are always later."

"Not this one," said Janna.

Frau Kopp looked at her suspiciously, opened her mouth to say something, and then closed it again. It was not wise to tangle with the Youth groups; she'd heard stories...Adjusting her black shawl, she shrugged her shoulders. "All right, go if you must and leave me with all the work." She bent and made a grab at the unsuspecting Lieschen. Janna lifted her coat from a nail and fled.

It was the last half of February. The thick blanket of snow was raveled and torn, showing patches of earth and yellow vegetation. Streams rushed singing down the hills, sweeping mud and pebbles along. The mountains, wrapped in fog, loomed like ghosts. Janna's boots picked up the sticky snow as she clumped along. A stiff wind tore at her hair and slapped her cheeks. She passed Frau Kopp's farmhouse with its steep, overhanging roof, half straw, half shingle. Bruno, the mongrel dog, almost choked himself on his chain trying to get to her. She patted his shaggy head, climbed a fence, and stood on the road, where puddles gleamed between ridges of mud. In the distance the church steeple lifted a warning finger at a flock of crows that seemed to be weaving swastikas against the sky.

Janna took a deep breath. She had managed to evade the cruel task Frau Kopp had laid on her because she was a Hitler Youth. Frau Kopp was afraid of Hitler. All grownups were.

She thought about the play again, still wondering at her luck to be chosen for such a big role when she was only a junior. Of course it was a responsibility too. Her mother always said that to be good you had to *live* the part. Janna tried to imagine herself as Brunhilde while she trudged along the sleety road...Brunhilde the Valkyrie, flying through the sky on a magic horse with her sisters, wearing full armor, with helmets on their streaming hair and spears in their hands. They directed all battles, taking care that the just won. Sometimes, when clouds massed on the horizon and Janna looked through her eyelashes, she fancied she saw them. They were warrior maidens, pure and immaculate. No one could touch them, they were free as the wind. If she were really Brunhilde, thought Janna, she'd be rid of grownups who always made her do what they wanted, who had their own kind of magic. She thought about Gisela in the village.

Last year she'd been in school, doing lessons like everyone else. Now she was grown up, wore pretty dresses, and walked like a queen. Any boys or men still left in the village flocked around her. People thought she was beautiful, but Janna didn't like her fat lips and the way she flapped her eyelashes. She was cruel too, often teasing her admirers. Janna hoped she wouldn't be like that when she grew up. It was better to be a Valkyrie, proud and stern, wielding a spear.

But Brunhilde disobeyed Wotan, the chief god, who wanted her to back the wrong side in a fight. Wotan punished her by chaining her to a rock in the middle of a ring of fire. There she had to sleep till Siegfried woke her. When he did, she went all soft and loved him. Janna wasn't sure she'd be able to lie absolutely still, without blinking. She wondered who would play the noble blond hero who had fearlessly slain a dragon yet trembled at the sight of Brunhilde's beauty. And that was another problem: Janna knew she was no beauty. Well, maybe they could do things with stage lights.

What would it be like to have a magic ring that gave you power over everybody? thought Janna. And why hadn't Brunhilde used it to save Siegfried and conquer her enemies? Why had she given it back to the Rhine maidens? They had hidden the ring and now no one could get it, though some people said it had been given to Hitler and that that was why he had conquered all those countries.

A girl hailed Janna from a neighboring farm. She came running across the fields, darting around rocks and shrubs, her long braids dancing on her back. It was Greta, a classmate.

"Wait for me, Janna!"

"You got away early too," said Janna.

"I lied, I said we had a Youth meeting."

"So did I!" The girls burst into laughter.

"They'll think it's funny when we have our rehearsal on Friday. They'll say we have too many special meetings!"

"They can't do anything," said Greta. "We're allowed as many meetings as we like."

"As long as our group leader doesn't tell on us."

"She won't. Hildegarde is nice. The other group leader we had, Hannelore, was awful, really strict. She used to make us march with heavy packs and take cold baths in freezing weather because she said we should be as tough as the boys. We were going to be the mothers of future German soldiers and she wasn't having any weaklings."

"Did you bag anything today?" asked Janna.

"Not much. I think Frau Hahn is noticing. But if she says anything, I'll tell on her. I'll tell she slaughtered a pig illegally."

"Did she?" asked Janna.

"Of course. They're always doing it, those farmers. They don't care if our soldiers starve. I got some onions anyway. They're good in soup."

"I got an egg," said Janna.

"An egg? But they count those!" exclaimed Greta.

"I got it before it was counted." They walked for a moment in silence, listening to a robin chirping on a bare branch.

The old mailman, his brown leather bag over his shoulder, was bicycling past. He was bent over the handlebars against the wind, treading down the pedals heavily with his big boots. Slush sprayed up and the girls jumped back.

"Grüss Gott!" said the mailman, nodding at them.

"Heil Hitler!" answered the girls, arms outstretched. Janna thoughtfully picked her way among the puddles.

"Did you ever see Hitler?" she asked.

"Yes, once," said Greta, "at that Youth rally we went to."

"There were too many people, I couldn't see a thing."

"I climbed a tree," said Greta, enjoying Janna's look of admiration. "But I didn't see much," she confessed. "Only the back of his head and his raised arm. And do you know, he didn't raise it high enough, not even as high as his shoulder!" Hildegarde made the girls raise their arms well above their heads, and no matter how long the occasion lasted, you were never allowed to rest your arm on the girl in front.

But of course Hitler didn't have to raise his arm at all; the greeting was *to* him. Besides, laws were for other people, not for Hitler.

"Why did *you* want to go home early today?" Janna asked.

"Because of the test tomorrow," said Greta, looking worried. "They keep us working so late, I'm too tired to do my homework. I did badly all this term. Race science is our most important subject and I want to do as well as I can, but I can't memorize all that stuff. Those terribly long words!"

"I know, like 'brachycephalic.' " said Janna. "That's a kind of skull. There are round, square, and long ones, and it's very important which kind you have. The Aryan ones are the best."

"Why?"

"It has something to do with room for your brains. Monkeys don't have much. Aryans have the most. We're Aryans, the only true race. We're supposed to become supermen."

"What other races are there?"

"Oh, Slavs and Mongolians and Semites…that's the Jews. When you don't know the answer to a question, just say something bad about the Jews and they'll give you a good mark. They'll forget what they asked."

"Really?"

"Sure, I tried it. It sometimes works with Slavs too, they're almost as bad as the Jews…that's the Russians, you know. But the Jews are the worst. They made us lose the First World War. We were winning the war, the soldiers were winning it—and Hitler was a soldier then so he knows—but the Jews in Berlin made us sign the Treaty of Versailles and that made us lose the war. We lost a lot of territory so we hadn't enough *Lebensraum* and we had to pay so much money to our enemies that we became poor. We even used our paper money in the toilets!"

"Why?" asked Greta.

"Because it was worth less than toilet paper. No one had work and people fell dead in the streets with hunger, but the democratic government did nothing. When Hitler came, he got back our lost territories and everyone had work. We had an army again and enough food. That's why we have to thank Hitler before and after meals."

"But what has that got to do with race?"

"Don't you see, Greta? It's race that makes the Jews so bad. They've got the wrong blood. We were pure Aryans before the Jews came and we must become pure Aryans again. That's why our boys have written on their daggers: 'Blood and honor.' It's shameful to let your race deteriorate by mixing it with inferior races. In the ancient days of Atlantis the Aryans had magic powers. The swastika is a magic Aryan sign, you know. But the Jews have weakened us and we've lost those powers. Hitler wants to give them back to us, but he can do it only if we stamp out the evil influence of the Jews."

"Did you ever see a Jew?" asked Greta.

"No, only in pictures."

"A Jew used to visit our village before you came," said Greta. "Every Friday he stood in the marketplace, selling a pig. He had a big yellow star on his coat. But there was always something wrong with the pig. We were glad when he didn't come any more."

"I think they're like the *Nibelungen* dwarfs in our play...sly and dangerous," said Janna. "It's the Jews in England and America that are fighting us. All the Aryan people would like to belong to us. And the Jews gave us Christianity, which is making us weak. Christians have to love their enemies, do good to those who hate them, and give more to those who steal from them. If you believe that, how can you be a strong nation and conquer the world? Hitler says it's impossible to be a good German and a Christian at the same time."

"Do you believe that?" asked Greta.

"Hitler says so," said Janna.

"And why are the Slavs bad?"

"They're Communists; the Jews gave them Communism. They say that everyone is equal, and that's a lie. There's a master race, that's us, and inferior races. The inferior races must serve the master race."

"You make it sound so simple, Janna. I wonder how you do it...all those long chapters in *Mein Kampf*..."

"I suppose it's because of my parents," said Janna. "They're famous, you know. Hitler said..."

"Yes, you told me," Greta broke in. The only thing she disliked about Janna was the way she boasted about her parents. "Here's my road. See you tomorrow."

Greta lived in a hut in the mountains, while Janna's home was in the village with her nurse Erna and Erna's mother. The celebrated Mechtild and Otto Oster, Janna's parents, had been traveling about for over two years, entertaining troops in foreign countries. They kept writing Janna that they would get a house soon and send for her, but so far it hadn't happened. Janna consoled herself by writing them long letters and talking about them to anyone who would listen. They were always present to her, an admiring audience for all she did.

Erna took great interest in Janna's Youth meetings, but the old mother, who mumbled away her last days in a rocking chair beside the huge blue porcelain stove, a rosary in perpetual motion between her fingers, disapproved of the Youth movement. She said it was wicked to hold meetings on Sunday mornings so that Janna could not go to church. She warned Janna not to listen to the pagan things she was being taught. She would go on to mutter threats against a mysterious being called Antichrist and predict all manner of evil for Germany, till Erna made her be quiet.

"Don't mind her," Erna would say contemptuously. "The old one is crazy."

Janna loved her Youth group. It was the only pleasant thing in her life. All the rest was grim. School from eight to twelve, much of the time taken up preparing bandages or doing other work for the soldiers, as well as writing letters to them. Then midday dinner, which consisted of potatoes with a flavor of meat. Then farm work in the afternoons. When there was no Youth meeting, Janna often had to work late, so that her homework suffered. The farmers forgot how young their helpers were and they piled on the work. If it had not been for the Hitler Youth, Janna didn't think she could have stood it.

The Youth meetings were delightful—except for readings from *Mein Kampf* or lectures on early Germanic tribes, which were dull. But the girls also learned handicrafts, practiced on musical instruments, played games, acted in plays, held songfests, and went on hikes. In the summer there were camping trips and excursions to Youth rallies. Those were the high points. When Janna was on a camping trip with her group, she felt confident, strong, and alive. The fresh air, the lovely woods and mountains, the comradeship of the other girls: it was glorious. They all felt they mattered, their country needed them—and what a beautiful, beautiful country it was!

In the evenings, tired out, they would gather around a leaping bonfire. Then Hildegarde would tell stories: old tales grown from the soil they sat on. They heard of the great Norse gods and their fiery matings, of curses and spells, of heroes with magic powers and of their malicious foes...till their eyelids pricked and the fire dwindled to a few glimmering worms. Then the night wind would blow them into their tents to dream of blond gods.

Janna loved it all. She sang enthusiastically with the rest:

> *"Today we own Germany,*
> *Tomorrow the world."*

She was nearing the village and looked forward to Erna's face when she saw the egg. Erna would tell her to thank Frau Kopp. Janna grinned. Frau Kopp would as soon part with her false teeth as with her eggs!

She had passed the first pastel-colored village houses with their wooden latticework, smoke curling from their chimneys. Usually Hans, the shoemaker, sat in front of his window, nodding at her, but today the window was empty. A bit farther on lived the clockmaker. His shop was full of interesting, carved wooden clocks, ticking and wheezing away, but Janna did not linger to look. She saw an ambulance standing before the little hotel. Frau Bauer, the hotelkeeper's wife, was opening the door for two men, who were carrying out Frau Bauer's old aunt on a stretcher. She was covered with a blanket and her face looked pale and anxious as she clutched the blanket with emaciated fingers.

"Now remember, Aunt Hedwig, it's for your own good. They are going to make you better," said Frau Bauer.

"I know…" quavered Aunt Hedwig. "They have this new treatment… but…"

"You don't want to go on having those pains," said Frau Bauer.

"But it's so far…" complained Aunt Hedwig. "You won't be able to visit me!"

"I wouldn't be able to anyway. The hotel…"

"I know, I know…" Aunt Hedwig's voice trailed off.

A group of villagers had gathered around the ambulance. The men carrying the stretcher had no expression on their faces. They did not talk to Aunt Hedwig or to Frau Bauer. They waited till the goodbyes were over; then they pushed the stretcher into the ambulance and slammed the doors shut. They climbed into the front seat. A stink came from the exhaust pipe as the ambulance sputtered into action, its wheels spraying slush, and growled off. The villagers watched it getting smaller and smaller till it disappeared down the hill. Frau Bauer sobbed and hurried into the hotel, her handkerchief pressed against her face.

"If she had to have new treatment, why not send her to the hospital in Freiburg? Why to Hadamar? It's so far away," said a woman.

"I think that's decided by the government," another voice remarked.

"Hadamar is for the aged and for incurables and feeble-minded," said Hans, the shoemaker. "It's a special place."

"That's true," the postmistress chipped in. "My sister's boy wasn't right in the head and they took him there, but he died soon after. They said it was pneumonia."

"Grandpa went there with a sore foot, and he died of pneumonia too," said a messenger boy. "It must be drafty in that place."

"He was old; perhaps the change was too much for him."

"Maybe," said the postmistress grimly. "But has any of you ever heard of anyone who came back from Hadamar alive?"

There was a silence. Somewhere a radio blared:

"Adolf Hitler's favorite flower
Is the simple edelweiss."

Janna shivered. Was something wrong? Was something dreadful going to happen to Aunt Hedwig? Gentle Aunt Hedwig, always lying on her long chair in front of the window and welcoming children with a box of homemade candy. She had been like a grandmother to Janna, telling her stories of long ago, when women wore long skirts and men had whiskers. Together they had pored over albums with stiff pages full of dried ferns and faded brown snapshots. If Aunt Hedwig had been in pain she had never shown it.

The tall youth standing beside Janna saw her distress. He belonged to the Jung Volk, the older boys' group. His name was Kurt Engel.

"Don't listen to those gossips," he said, putting his hand on Janna's shoulder as he walked beside her. That was a great honor.

"Do you think she'll be all right?" asked Janna timidly, gazing up at him. Kurt looked away into the distance. The main street was sloping down steeply now, and they could see the misted valley with row upon row of snowcapped mountains melting into a haze of purple.

"Does it matter?" he asked. "Aunt Hedwig is a useless old woman of no further value to our nation. Why worry about her? Don't you realize what is happening to our young people, our soldiers in Russia? Have you seen the list of the dead? Why don't you worry about them?" He was gazing at the sky where the last rays of the sun slanted down like spears from a gap in the clouds.

"We're in a crisis," he said. "Only four times in history was there a similar crisis in Europe: when the Greeks warded off the Persians, when Charles Martel defended France against Islam, when Vienna held out against the Turks, and when the Teutonic knights stopped the hordes of Genghis Khan at Liegnitz. Now, once again Europe is threatened by barbarians from the East and we Germans are called to save it." Kurt's closely cropped head, lifted against the sky, looked stern and noble, thought Janna.

"There is a prophecy," Kurt went on, "that after the gods were killed, the horn of Heimdall, the guardian of the border line between gods and men, would sound one day to awaken the Germanic race. I think it has happened: Hitler is that horn. He has special powers and is sent to lead us to a great victory, which will be spoken of for centuries to come. We must trust him and follow him, even unto death."

"Oh, I hope not *death*," cried Janna.

Kurt looked down at her as if he had just discovered her. His smile lit up his face. "You're all right, Janna," he said. "Don't worry. Hitler is invincible, a man of destiny. With him we can do anything. See you Friday. I suppose you know I'm playing Siegfried..." Nodding affably at her, he strode off, tall and handsome in his leather jacket. Janna stared after him. So *he* was to be Siegfried! What a stunning Siegfried he would make! She began to think about her costume: a flowing white dress with silver breastplates, a girdle studded with jewels, and a helmet on her head. She also needed silver sandals and a spear. She wondered where she'd get all that, but Hildegarde would help, she always did. Janna was almost home before she remembered the egg.

"See what I've got for you, Erna!" she cried, bursting into the kitchen. Erna looked around. She was, holding a letter.

"Janna!" she exclaimed, scarcely noticing the egg. "I'm so glad you are early! We just got this special-delivery letter. Your father and mother have found a house in Amsterdam. They want you to join them as soon as possible. You'll be traveling with a Frau Mueller, an officer's wife who is visiting her husband. So much to do, I don't know where to start! But... what's the matter? Don't you *want* to go to your parents?"

Crossing the Rhine

Janna trudged along the platform beside Frau Mueller, a thin, nervous woman who kept asking questions without listening to the answers. Janna had already told her three times that yes, she was glad to be going to her parents, and no, she had never visited Holland before.

"You'll like it," Frau Mueller promised. "Wait till I fix this parcel, it keeps slipping. Oh, could you? Thanks, that's better." For Janna, who carried only a small suitcase and a bag, had relieved her of some of her packages.

"You can't get anything in the Dutch shops any more," Frau Mueller complained. "The few things that are left are all imitation, just as over here. In 1940, ah, what riches! What luxuries! Things we hadn't seen here for *years!* But that is all over now," she ended sadly.

They were walking alongside a dingy-looking train with a clumsy, wood-burning engine. The Freiburg station was like a madhouse: people running about, people embracing, people sitting patiently on suitcases, porters shouting at everybody to get out of the way. There were many soldiers with duffel bags. The train was packed. People were standing in the aisles, but at the very back Frau Mueller managed to find an almost empty car. It was filling up last because it was unheated. It was also dirty and had a damp smell. The floor had not been swept, newspapers lay about, and several windowpanes were broken. Frau Mueller chose two opposite window seats near the door to the next compartment. She began to distribute her luggage in the overhead racks. Janna noticed the name Edeltraut Mueller on the labels. So she was called Edeltraut. Grownups should not have first names, thought Janna. It made them ridiculous. Except royalty, of course, or actors.

"I hope we won't be bombed," said Edeltraut Mueller, pushing one of her parcels farther back.

"Bombed?" asked Janna.

"Yes, the last time I went to Amsterdam we had to get out of the train and take shelter in a ditch. Glass got sprayed all over my best suit. I could never wear it again. Some people were killed."

This was a shock to Janna. It was all right to sit on a plush seat in a movie theater and watch your own heroic pilots bombing foreign cities. It was quite different, somehow, when it happened to you. She looked around. The carriage was filling up with soldiers. Good, they would protect her.

A fat man, loaded with luggage, came waddling up the aisle. Besides his bulging suitcases he was carrying an armload of blankets. Around his body hung various leather cases on straps. A Tyrolean hat perched rakishly on his head, belying his glowering face. He made a crash landing beside Janna, who was almost bounced out of her seat. The fat man took no notice of her or of Frau Mueller. He muttered something about the cold and began to wrap himself methodically in his blankets. He noticed a draft coming through the broken window beside Janna and pointed to it.

"Stuff up that hole," he commanded. "I've got delicate lungs." Janna had been taught to be obliging, so she picked up one of the newspapers, gritty with dirt, and plugged up the hole. A few slivers of glass broke off, but she finally got the paper to stick. She cut her finger and sucked it noisily. The fat man took no notice. He didn't even say "Thank you." He had swaddled himself so completely that he seemed to be in a cocoon, with only his nose sticking out. It was a fat, purplish nose and Janna pictured herself knitting a pink cozy for it. That made her laugh. With difficulty the fat man wrenched his face toward her and snarled, "Children shouldn't be seen or heard."

Janna thought that too much, after what she had just done for him. She sucked harder on her finger in protest.

It was indeed cold in the carriage. It looked as if the passengers were all smoking; their breath came in clouds. The soldiers, warmly dressed, were laughing and joking.

Frau Mueller produced a blanket for herself and a pillow. She did not offer to share them with Janna. While she was settling herself, her foot accidentally hit the fat man's. He barked immediately, "Woman, mind what you're doing!"

Just before the train started, a little man edged in and sat down in the only vacant seat, beside Frau Mueller and opposite the fat man. He was clasping a scuffed imitation-leather briefcase. His coat had a turned-up collar, which hid his mouth and chin, while his wide-brimmed hat shaded his forehead and eyes. All you could see was a slightly arched nose. The toes of his boots curled up, showing worn soles. He sat on the edge of his seat as if ready to jump up the next moment. He greeted Janna, the fat man, and Frau Mueller with timid nods. When the train pulled out of the station, he relaxed slightly and blew his nose.

The fat man kept staring rudely at him. At last he rasped, "Why aren't you wearing your star?" The little man sat up straight, his eyes widening. A hush came over the coach. Janna felt furious. Only Jews wore stars. "Don't mind him," she said to the little man. "He has been insulting all of us."

Now the fat man turned his attention to her again. "You are the most insufferable brat it has ever been my misfortune to meet," he growled. "I don't know what your mother is thinking of, letting you grow up with such objectionable manners!" He glared at Frau Mueller, who hastily disclaimed any relationship.

"She isn't my daughter; I am only looking after her for the trip."

"Then why don't you do it?" the fat man asked. "Shut her up." Frau Mueller sputtered as she took up her knitting.

Janna turned in disgust to the window and watched the fleeing landscape. The smoke of the engine streamed past like the tail of a runaway horse. Behind it rose and dipped the dappled beauty of the mountains. Her dear, dear Black Forest! How she hated to leave it! Tears came into her eyes as she remembered parting that morning with Hildegarde and the rest of the group. Even Kurt had come, briefly, on his bicycle, to take leave of her.

"Tough luck..." he had said. "I was looking forward to seeing more of you." He had put his hand on her shoulder for a moment. "Chin up," he had added, with his dazzling smile. "Don't forget us!"

Hildegarde had been most gracious. Janna had cried a bit as she told the leader how she'd miss being in the play. "Yes, it's a shame," Hildegarde admitted, handing her a package. "But never mind, you can be a Brunhilde in real life, that's even better." When Janna opened the package, she found a lovely book with colored illustrations and the text of the *Nibelungen* operas. She flung her arms around Hildegarde's neck and kissed her.

"I'm glad you like it," Hildegarde said. "It seemed such a shame for you to have to go just now. I thought it might help."

"Oh, it does! It does! I've never had such a beautiful book!" After that Greta had been shy about her own little gift, a homemade penwiper. But Janna kissed her too and thanked her just as much. Greta could not help it that her parents were not rich like Hildegarde's. The whole group had seen her to the bus stop. Erna had gone with Janna to Freiburg to meet Frau Mueller.

It seemed to Janna that she had been traveling for a long time already, but there was still an eight-hour journey ahead of her. Her body was being hurried forward while her mind lagged behind, clinging to her friends. When would she see them again?

Janna had insisted on wearing her Youth uniform, which was the nicest thing she had: a dark woolen skirt buttoned to a white blouse, and a black kerchief pulled through a real leather ring. Her coat covered it, but it made her feel more confident. They'd be starting rehearsals tomorrow; someone else would be Brunhilde, probably that stuck-up Ilse. Janna closed her eyes, feeling a stab of misery.

Wave upon wave of mountains passed as Janna brooded. She reminded herself that she was going home to the wonderful parents she had been telling everyone about. But as the train brought her nearer and nearer to them, misgivings crowded her mind. Did she remember them properly? It seemed so long since she had seen them. She tried to think back, but the more she tried, the more unreal they became. As she thought about the old days in Berlin, all she could remember were long periods when her parents were on tour and she and Erna were left alone in the gloomy flat with the heavy velvet draperies and the large, round, gold-framed mirrors decorated with eagles. With an effort, she remembered parties: the rooms lit up and buzzing with visitors, servants hurrying back and forth with trays—Janna dressed up and presented to nice-smelling ladies who kissed her…

"She's not a bit like you, is she, Mechtild? Much more like her father…" Laughter… Sometimes concerts to which she and Erna listened, sitting at the top of the stairs…

On St. Nicholas Eve, the fifth of December, there was always a special party for Janna. Then St. Nicholas, dressed in purple robes, came to the flat. The family and their guests awaited him in the living room, forming a semicircle with Janna and Erna in front. St. Nicholas would ask if she had been good, and to Janna's horror Erna would betray Janna's most shameful secrets: that she had wet her bed, told lies, and sucked her thumb. St. Nicholas then beat her with a switch in which candies were hidden. The harder he beat her, the more sugarplums fell out. It made the grownups laugh very much, but it hurt—and once Janna had refused to pick up the candies afterward and had been carried to bed in disgrace.

Why did these silly incidents come into her mind? Why couldn't she remember her parents helping her with her homework or taking her for walks? Had she a bad memory, or...or...were they not really a proper family? She had always been with Erna. This was the first time she had been away from her. Maybe that was making her feel strange. She was older now, almost twelve. Her parents would treat her more like an equal. They knew everything about her, she had written them so many letters. Reassured, she felt her eyelids close... she'd started *very* early that morning...

She woke up because Frau Mueller shook her.

"The *Rhine*," she said. "You must look at the *Rhine*." Janna saw a fairy-tale river flowing between high mountains dotted with castles. The Rhine! The abode of the Rhine maidens, who had owned the gold which the Nibelung dwarf stole to make his magic ring. There was a picture of them in her book. She took it out of her bag and leafed through it. Yes, there they were, pale and translucent, dancing on a wave, their arms lifted, their hair flowing. Beautiful.

The Rhine was an especially German river. Many tales and legends were connected with it. Janna remembered Herr Schultz, the geography teacher, telling the class, "Because the Rhine starts in Switzerland and ends in Holland, those countries really belong to us."

Janna felt hungry. She was glad when she saw people opening their lunch boxes. The fat man had wriggled out of his cocoon and was eating bread and sausage, washed down with beer. Most people had only meager provisions. Janna herself had two cheese sandwiches and an apple. She ate slowly to make them last. Frau Mueller had unpacked buns, cakes, hard-boiled eggs, and a flask of coffee. The little man beside her must be hungry, for his nostrils seemed to twitch as the delicious smells of Frau Mueller's meal wafted past him. But he sat motionless, his hands tightly clasped, his eyes cast down. He had no lunch, that was obvious. Looking at him, Janna could not enjoy hers. And there was Frau Mueller with oceans of food, gorging beside him. It made Janna mad. Closing her eyes, she *willed* Frau Mueller to share her food with the little man. But when she opened them, Frau Mueller was still placidly chewing, her jaws working, the long hair on her chin wiggling. As she swallowed her coffee, her Adam's apple bobbed up and down. How could she be so selfish? There was only one thing left for Janna to do.

"Here," she said, thrusting her second sandwich at the little man. "I have two." The little man came alive. He grabbed the sandwich. "Thank you," he said hoarsely. In a few seconds the sandwich was gone. Now Janna could finish her own meal.

The fat man had taken no notice of the transaction. He was too intent on spreading smelly cheese over crackers.

The train was now speeding through a settled part of the country. In Mainz, Janna saw that many houses were in ruins.

"What happened?" she cried. People left their seats to look.

"Don't you know?" asked Frau Mueller. "Don't you read the papers? That's the work of our enemies. You see what barbarians they are, bombing helpless women and children." It was an appalling sight. Houses gaped like rotten teeth. Here and there wisps of smoke still wandered over the ruins, like ghosts. There were pathetic remnants of furniture: a picture on a crumbling wall, patches of flowered wallpaper, a cradle hanging drunkenly from a rafter. There was a stench of burning.

"Why don't we stop them?" asked Janna. "Aren't we winning?"

"Of course we're winning," snapped Frau Mueller. "Gustav, my husband, says it is only a matter of months. If the English had surrendered like the other countries, we'd all be better off. Now Hitler will destroy them, and America too. He has a secret weapon, you know."

"Pardon me," said the fat man disagreeably. "If you have such important information, you should keep your mouth shut."

"Everybody knows it," Frau Mueller answered defensively.

"Then there is even less need to mention it."

"It gives people courage," argued Frau Mueller.

"Only fools are encouraged by hearing of a weapon that is not being used," sneered the fat man.

"If it isn't finished yet…"

"Then it might come too late." And the fat man gave a ghoulish chuckle. Janna had been listening with growing annoyance. The fat man did not seem to care what happened to his country. He could not be a good German. Perhaps he was a spy, or… a smuggler! It wasn't really cold enough to cover up. Janna wondered whether the fat man was hiding something.

The little man was sitting as straight as ever, hugging his briefcase. He had picked up one of the newspapers and he ducked behind it every time the train stopped at a station. For a while the only sound in the carriage was the hum of the wheels and the snores of sleeping passengers. They had passed Koblenz. The afternoon sun slanted across the fields, painting long shadows. Janna leafed through her book, reading bits here and there. She began to nod over the pages. She did not know how long she had dozed when a cry from the passengers aroused her. The train was slowly chugging through a desert of rubble. No house stood upright. Only the Cologne Cathedral rose proudly above the ruins. There was a hush after the outcry. Cologne gone… the *whole* city!

"I heard there had been bombing," said Frau Mueller. "But I did not know it was this bad!" Janna clenched her fists. Hitler was right to fight the monsters who did such things.

When the train reached the bridge over the Rhine, a warning voice sounded from carriage to carriage: "Shut the windows, shut the windows." No one had been so foolish as to open one in Janna's carriage. It was bad enough to have the cold air whistling through the cracks.

"Why do they say that?" Janna asked. Frau Mueller pointed to the notice which informed passengers that they were to close their windows when crossing the Rhine. "In case of violation," it said, "the soldiers have orders to make use of their guns." Janna looked at the soldiers in the carriage, but none of them seemed interested in his gun.

"Why?" she asked.

The fat man turned on her. "Always asking questions," he scolded. "You're supposed to do as you're told without asking why. If you weren't such a little fool, you'd see that an enemy could throw a bomb through an open window and blow up the bridge."

"He'd blow up the train too, then, and himself," Janna pointed out.

"Never heard of Samson?" asked the fat man.

"No," said Janna. "Who is he?"

"Never mind," said the fat man. "Now shut up, I want my nap."

Janna kept her eyes on him. She did not trust him. He might be only pretending to sleep and suddenly jump up, pulling a bomb from under his wraps. But they reached the other side of the Rhine without mishap. The landscape looked as if someone had ironed it. Gone were all the hills or hillocks. The sky arched vast and endless. Little houses huddled under little trees, trying to escape the threat of the black clouds that were massing on the horizon. Janna watched the clouds creeping nearer and nearer; soon they would blot out the sun. Harsh voices in the next coach warned the travelers that train control was on the way. Everyone braced themselves for the ordeal. Janna's papers were in order. As a Hitler Youth she had no fears, but Frau Mueller was fidgeting. She had lost her ticket and, made nervous by the obvious interest of the fat man, ransacked her possessions. She finally found it with gusty relief, disappointing the fat man.

Everywhere people were searching their inside pockets, wallets, and handbags. As the officials entered, all chatter stopped. They walked to the rear of the car and started there. They looked at identification papers, work permits, travel permits, tickets, and passports. They asked if anyone had cameras or other forbidden articles. No one reported any. The officials lingered for a while by some ill-dressed, lean young men who said they were Dutch labor draftees on a visit to their parents. After a lot of questions the officials passed on. The little man was growing paler as they approached. While they were questioning the fat man, the little man began to tremble. His hand shook as he held out his passport and identification papers.

"I'd take a good look at those, Officers," said the fat man with a grin as he whisked his own credentials back into the folds of his blankets. "I should imagine they are forged."

"Take off your hat," the officials told the little man, comparing his face with the passport photo. Janna suddenly saw what the fat man was up to. That's why he had hoped Frau Mueller had lost her ticket. He wanted attention diverted from himself. She pointed to the fat man.

"He is only saying that because he is a smuggler himself," she shouted. "He wasn't telling the truth when he said he had no cameras. He has several. I saw them before he put on those blankets!"

The officials flung the little man's papers back at him and pounced on the fat man, whose cheeks turned purple with rage.

"I am an important person," he blustered. "You fools, you don't know what you're doing. You're obstructing the affairs of the nation. You'll suffer for it!"

The officers were peeling him like an onion, and not too gently. They did not like being threatened or called fools. They were used to obsequious submission.

Janna had guessed right. The various leather cases contained expensive cameras and other photographic equipment.

"I'm a professional free-lance photographer. I've done work for Göring and I've a right to carry these," said the fat man, trying to control his temper.

"It doesn't say anything about that in your papers," the officers pointed out sternly. "All it says is that you are going to work for an art dealer in Amsterdam."

"Yes, I take photographs for reproductions. Is that so strange?" the fat man said. He was sweating.

"Oh, very neat," praised the officials. "Why did you not tell us that right away? Why didn't you declare the cameras?"

"Because I've mislaid my confounded permit," exploded the fat man. "That can happen, to anyone, can't it? I just couldn't find it... and the train wouldn't wait. I knew I'd have trouble with you people, you vultures in uniform, always happy to peck at your betters over some trifle..."

"That's enough," said the officials. "You can explain all that at the police station." Now the fat man really got angry and became so abusive that the officers began to think he must be an escaped lunatic. They put handcuffs on him and took him off the train, trailing his blankets.

The little man, forgotten now, put down his newspaper and leaned back limply, with closed eyes.

Janna felt elated. She had *done* it. She had captured a smuggler! Maybe she could be Brunhilde in real life, as Hildegarde had said. She must write and tell Hildegarde about it. There were moments when flashes of fear pricked her self-satisfaction: what would have happened if those leather cases had held only shoe polish? Nor could she forget the fat man's face as he snarled at her, "You obnoxious, meddlesome brat, I'll pay you back for this," before he was dragged off. But she consoled herself with the thought that he would be locked up and unable to carry out his threat.

She watched the snowy fields, spread out like handkerchiefs. The clouds had gobbled up the sky now and it was beginning to snow. At a red-brick building the train stopped and went backward, as if reluctant to cross the border. Then, with a spurt, it entered Dutch territory. Immediately the rhythm of the wheels changed from clack...clack... clack...to clickety-clackety. They passed a freight train with a long row of cattle cars. Janna had seen similar ones before. She had seen the wet straw in them and had smelled the stench of urine. She had seen cows herded through the open doors. But the doors in these cars were not only shut but padlocked, and at intervals armed guards stood on the roofs. Out of the small, barred windows peered faces, human faces.

Something froze in Janna as she saw the closed wagons rattle and swoosh past: swoosh, swoosh, swoosh. More and more of them, an endless procession. And people, yes, *people* in all of them! White faces with dark, staring eyes.

"There are *people* in there," she cried, and some of the horror she felt spilled over in her voice. "There are *people* in there! What's going to happen to them?"

"Hush," said Frau Mueller. "Hold your tongue, child. It's a cattle train," and she pulled down the shade so that Janna could not see any more. "You are imagining things."

"I am *not* imagining things. There *were* people in it…" Janna repeated. The coach was silent. Everyone seemed to have drawn a blind in front of their face and disappeared behind it. Only the little man lifted his head and looked at Janna. The suffering in his eyes made her own fill with tears. And so they looked at each other, Janna and the little man, and they seemed the only ones alive, in the coach.

The Arrival

Later there were delays. The train stopped at Amersfoort. All the passengers had to transfer to another train, and in the shuffle Janna lost sight of the little man.

It was dark when they arrived in Amsterdam. Janna's parents were waiting for her in the dimly lit Central Station. Frau Mueller delivered Janna to them and hurried off to her husband. Janna stood facing her parents. They seemed unreal until they spoke. Then their voices brought a flood of memories and Janna flung herself into their arms.

"Thank God, we have our daughter back," her father said. "Welcome to Amsterdam." As he kissed her, Janna smelled the familiar odor of makeup. Then it was her mother's turn. "Janna, darling," she sang, pressing her daughter to her fur coat. "Is it really *you*, at last?" Other people were pushing past them, jostling them, until Frau Oster's melodious German sentences rose above the hubbub. Then, suddenly, there was an empty space around them.

"It's been so *long*," Janna's mother wailed. "At last I could not bear it any more. I told the Baron that he'd better do something and he did. Wait till you see the house. It's *superb*!"

"The Baron's car is waiting outside," said Herr Oster, picking up Janna's suitcase. "Is this all the luggage you have?"

"And this," said Janna, showing her small bag.

"But that's *nothing*," said her mother. "What can you have brought to wear? Did Erna use your clothes coupons for herself?" Janna flushed. Her attachment to Erna was more from habit than from genuine affection, but Erna had been good to her and she was part of Janna's life in the Black Forest.

"Oh no," she cried. "Erna wouldn't do that, she's very honest, but you could buy so little in the village and Erna was too tired to sew for me."

"Too lazy, you mean," corrected her father. "We paid her enough! Never mind, that deal is off now." He was hurrying after the crowd through a tunnel. Janna and her mother had to run to keep up with him.

"No, no," Janna panted. "Erna was not lazy…she had a lot…to… do… She took in washing and her mother was old…often ill…" But her father was not listening.

They reached the exit, where Janna handed her ticket to the collector. From the station they stepped into the murky confusion of a blacked-out city. It was snowing and raining at the same time. A drizzly fog absorbed what glimmers of light there were. Passengers were dispersing in all directions. No one lingered. People shrugged up their collars, unfolded ragged umbrellas, or mounted rattling bicycles with wooden tires. The only car in sight was the Baron's Mercedes, waiting for the Osters. The chauffeur, who opened the door for them, tried to ignore the rude whistles of some urchins.

Janna sank gratefully into the rich upholstery of the car. She was still shivering after her cold journey. Frau Oster rubbed Janna's fingers between her soft, fragrant palms. "Poor lamb, you're frozen. Was it a terrible journey? I was so afraid you'd be bombed!"

The car began to crawl along the streets, its dimmed lights barely showing the way, making spooky ghosts of anyone they lit up. The windshield wiper creaked busily as wet snow kept slapping against the glass. Here and there the blue flashlight of a pedestrian wavered like a will-o'-the-wisp. There was a strong smell of dirty water.

"That's the canals," Janna's mother said in a low voice. "There are more here than in Venice. I hate them. You can hardly see them at night... especially in this weather. They have no guard rails. Many of our people have blundered into them."

"Been pushed in," said Herr Oster.

"Oh no, Otto!"

"When will you face the facts, Mechtild? The Dutch hate us. They are a dour, obstinate, cantankerous, inhospitable lot, and they hate our guts."

"Otto...mind the child."

"She may as well know what she's in for. I wasn't too keen on sending for her, remember? She was safer where she was." Frau Oster squealed as the car gave a sudden lurch.

"Otto, tell the chauffeur to be careful! Tell him to go slow. This is where the car drove into the canal last week and all the officers were drowned..."

"That was a bit farther on, and they were drunk," said Herr Oster. "It came out in the autopsy. You wouldn't have been so upset if they hadn't been friends of your baron."

Janna was peering into the gloom. She couldn't see anything. "There was a fat man in the train..." she began, wanting to tell her parents about her journey.

"Was there, dear?" said her mother. "What do you mean, *my* baron, Otto? He is yours too. What would we do without him?"

"And what will you do if he wants a return for his favors?" asked Herr Oster.

"I'll give him my autographed picture," said Mechtild lightly.

Otto burst into laughter. "You always were a devil, Mechtild!"

"And when the train control came..." Janna said for the third time.

"Yes, dear...Otto, shouldn't we turn left here?"

"He knows the way," Otto said.

"And when the train control came..." Janna repeated once more.

"I'm sure we should have turned left," said her mother.

"Mechtild, what are you worrying about? He knows these streets like the back of his hand by now."

"Not in this weather," said Frau Oster, shivering.

"They asked if anyone had a camera and he said he hadn't but…"

"There now! I told you!" The car had come to a sudden stop against a dark lamppost. The chauffeur was addressing an invisible pedestrian with an assortment of German curses. The pedestrian slunk off, but several snowballs thudded against the windows. The chauffeur backed carefully.

"The fat man tried to make the train officers suspect the little man. But I said he had cameras and then…" Janna went on doggedly. Her mother's eyes were straining into the darkness.

"Yes, darling… Otto… what is he doing now? Are you sure he knows the way? All these canals look alike."

"Calm down, Mechtild, we're here." The car stopped. Janna was helped out, feeling wet snowflakes in her face. They went down a few steps to a kind of basement door, which opened into a warm, dry, clean white-marble hall with a black-and-white tiled floor. A thin, frightened-looking maid took their coats, shaking them and hanging them in a closet. Janna followed her parents into the dining room, which was warmed by a coal stove. Vaguely she was aware of oak paneling, carved furniture, and a thick carpet, for her attention was caught by the supper spread on the dining table and lit by a hanging lamp. On the white tablecloth flowered dishes held a wide variety of food: pickled herring, slices of meat, homemade bread, and rich, yellow butter. While Janna was looking at the food, her parents were studying her.

"I thought she'd have grown tall and strong after more than two years in the country," Frau Oster said in a disappointed voice. "I think she has got a little taller, but so skinny! And her hair! What possessed Erna to let her scrape it away from her face like that, in tight braids? She used to have curls."

"I see you are a member of the Hitler Youth, Janna," said her father approvingly, noticing her uniform. Janna flashed him a smile.

"Heil Hitler!" she said, raising her arm as high as she could.

"Heil Hitler," answered her father, raising his. Janna looked at his slightly graying, curly black hair, his florid, handsome face and expressive brown eyes. He looked kind, but there was something stern about his lips and chin. Janna remembered being afraid of him as a small child. Her mother, beside him, looked frail and fluffy. Mechtild never seemed to age. Her hair threw a golden mist around her elfin face with its elusive, silver eyes.

Meanwhile, those eyes were taking in Janna's uniform. "You'd have thought," she said slowly, "that a Strength Through Joy movement, as it's supposed to be called, would have come up with something more cheerful. You look like a magpie in mourning." Tears sprang into Janna's eyes.

"It's a *good* uniform," she said hotly. "Pure wool, no imitation, not even the leather ring. The other girls envied me. And when we marched it looked...it looked..."

"Magnificent," her father said, finishing the sentence for her. "Of course it did. Your mother doesn't understand." He frowned at his wife, who waved an expressive hand.

"All right, come and eat, dears." They sat down. Janna felt ravenous. Her parents let her stuff herself in peace while they talked about their current play.

"If it weren't for you, it would have flopped," Otto said. "Such a dreary interpretation of the saga. Anything for novelty, I suppose."

"You do your share," said his wife, "though I wish you were my lover and not my husband." She added milk and water to his cup. "That Siegmund is so empty-headed."

"Well, he had to be your twin, and I suppose he was the only actor blond enough," said Otto tolerantly.

"You do the lover ever so much better."

"I've had practice," Otto said, smiling. "He is only a stripling, but he does match your general appearance. Those old folktales should not be put into modern dress, it takes away their glamour. That's especially true of the *Nibelungen* saga..."

"The *Nibelungen* saga?" Janna's head shot up, her eyes sparkled. "Are you playing in the *Nibelungen* saga? I am too...I was, I mean, if I hadn't come here. They gave me the part of Brunhilde and I'm not even a senior!" Her parents exchanged proud glances.

"Well, well," said her father, tweaking her ear. "You've inherited our curse...I guess you're doomed. You must act bits for us when we have time."

"Brunhilde, that was my first role," said her mother. "We must talk about it another day...but, if you've finished eating, we'd like you to tell us some things we have to know, since you're going to live with us." They started to ask her questions. Some of them puzzled Janna, for they could have got the answers out of her letters. She began to wonder whether they had received them. She had so much to tell them, but they kept wanting to hear stupid things like how often she'd been to the dentist, when she had been vaccinated last, and whether she had brought her school report.

"We'll have to see about schooling for you," her father said. "It's a bad situation at present. The teachers are uncooperative. And many schools are closed because of fuel shortages. I think the best thing would be to find you a tutor. Meanwhile, a little vacation won't do you any harm. You look as if you need it."

"Yes," said her mother eagerly. "We'll have to fatten you up! We have plenty of food, thanks to the Baron, though it's sometimes unusual food, whatever he manages to find. We enjoyed your letters, Janna. That Hildegarde you wrote about seems a nice girl. Was she in your class?" Janna stared at her. She had written over and over that Hildegarde was her group leader, so how could she be in Janna's class? She was much too old! Janna tried to explain this, but her mother said it was time for bed.

"Bed?" asked Janna. "But it isn't eight yet. At home I don't have to go till nine."

Her mother frowned. "This is your home now," she said. "And we make the rules here. You must be tired out after that long journey and I want to tuck you in before we have to leave for the theater."

The theater! Of course, Janna had forgotten. That was why she could not remember any family evenings, there hadn't been any. That was when her parents worked. Her lips trembled.

"Why did you let me come," she burst out, "if we're not going to be a proper family? If we're not going to be together, if you're going to be away all the time. There I had friends...I was going to be in the play..." Her mother shrank back, hurt.

Her father's voice came like a whiplash. "That's enough, Johanna. You do not talk like that to your mother, who was so anxious to have you and took such pains to get you here. Tell her you are sorry at once."

"I'm sorry, Mother." Janna's voice trembled. Her eyelids stung.

"It's all right, dear. You're overtired, I know."

"I'll carry her upstairs," said her father in a kinder tone. In his strong arms Janna was carried up the two flights of stairs to her room, as if she were still five years old. The room was pretty, with silver wallpaper, a frilled dressing table, and bright pictures on the walls. But what Janna noticed first was an enormous, old-fashioned wardrobe.

"My dresses will look silly in that..." she murmured sleepily. Frau Oster found Janna's nightgown and toothbrush in her bag.

"You can unpack your suitcase tomorrow," she said, helping Janna undress. Janna sank into the soft mattress, so unlike the straw one she was used to. Her mother tucked the fluffy blankets around her.

"Sleep well, Jannelein, there are lots of surprises awaiting you tomorrow. We haven't had time to tell you everything. We're so happy to have you back," she said, kissing Janna and flicking out the light.

Janna lay staring into the darkness. She knew she should be happy. This was a lovely house and her parents had been very kind. Yet she felt homesick. Not for the Black Forest, though she missed the scent of pine trees coming through her attic window, nor for Erna, though it seemed queer not to hear her rattling about in the kitchen and scolding her old mother... No, what made the tears come in the darkness was the loss of those perfect, devoted parents she had lived with the last two years, those parents who hung on her every word, who read and reread her letters, and spent the rest of the time talking about her, the parents to whom she had poured out her heart. They were gone. They had been chased away by the real ones, who had their own lives to live, their profession, and each other. They did not need Janna.

It made her feel as lonely as a pluck of sheep's wool on a barbed-wire fence. She groped for her uniform. Clasping it, she fell asleep.

The House

JANNA DREAMED THAT SHE WAS BRUNHILDE, but Wotan had sent her away in disgrace. The fat man had told him stories about her and he was very angry. Janna tried to make her horse fly, but it wouldn't. Its feet seemed glued to the ground. She tugged at the reins but it wouldn't go up...and it must, it must. They had to get away, for behind them the town was in flames. Only the cathedral still stood. All the houses were burning and white faces looked out of the windows. Swoosh, swoosh, went the flames.

Janna whipped her horse, terrified.

Wotan looked down at her and shook the clouds. Big hailstones fell out and exploded...bang...bang...bang...all around her.

Janna woke up, but the noise remained with her... There was a chattering of guns outside, a growling of airplanes, explosions. She cowered under the blankets, her fingers in her ears. Had the enemy come? Were they doing to Amsterdam what they had done to Cologne? Was she going to die...this minute? But she did not know how to die...she was not old enough. It wasn't fair. Yet it had happened to people in Cologne, in Mainz. There must have been girls like her, who did not know how to die...

The noise stopped. The drone of the airplanes dwindled and Janna went back to sleep.

When she opened her eyes the next morning, she expected to hear the crow of Erna's rooster and the sound of Erna raking the stove. Instead, there were street noises, a dog barking, children's voices. She was in Amsterdam! Hastily she slipped out of bed and pushed aside the thick blackout curtains.

What she had guessed to be windows were really glass doors opening onto a balcony. Beyond she saw a row of back gardens, separated by fences. The sun was shining on a dazzling white vista of snowy roofs, snow-trimmed trees, and distant, snow-capped spires. But thaw was already marring this beauty: drops from the roofs were pitting the snow on the balcony.

In the adjoining garden children were playing. They were making a snowman and their little dog was scurrying off with the pipe they wanted to put in his mouth. When they retrieved it, he grabbed the hat instead. There was a great deal of running, chasing, calling out, and laughter. The dog was called Fokkie. Janna watched for some time. Then, heedless of the cold, she opened the glass doors and called, "Hello!"

She expected the children to wave to her and greet her. Instead, they gave her a startled glance, whispered together a moment, and vanished into the house, the dog at their heels. Only the snowman was left, sagging a little, his pipe crooked, his hat over one eye. Footprints were scattered around him like confetti.

Janna shivered and closed the doors. She pulled at the string which opened the draperies, and sunlight came flooding into the room. It was even prettier by daylight. The wardrobe looked even larger. A whole family could hide in it, Janna thought. It was decorated with prettily carved animals and flowers, and hugged the wall so closely it might have grown together with it.

The rest of the room was dainty enough: it had a desk with a small statue on it of a praying child, flanked by two candlesticks, a bookcase filled with picture books, delicate watercolor paintings on the walls, and beside the bed a little white rocking chair with a blue cushion. Janna's eyes filled with tears. She felt remorse. She had misjudged her parents. They must love her very much to have spent so much thought and effort to get a room ready for her. She noticed a doll sprawling on top of the bookcase, an old doll that had lost its hair. The color had been washed out of its cheeks, but it smiled confidently, knowing its value. Janna touched it gingerly. She had never played with dolls... where had her parents got it?

When Janna returned from the bathroom, she unpacked her suitcase. She hadn't realized that her dresses were so shabby. In this room they looked like leftovers from a rummage sale, but she had to wear one, for her uniform was all wrinkled. She opened the wardrobe to hang up the others and she got a pleasant shock. It was not empty, as she had expected; it was full of pretty girl's clothes. That must be her mother's doing. She must have been shopping in the Black Market. Her parents must have become rich!

With a glow of gratitude, Janna lifted down one of the dresses and tried it on. It fitted snugly. Janna put the other things on in turn and they were all the right size. How clever of her mother! They were of better material and cut than Janna had been used to, though not quite new. Secondhand, probably.

She looked in the oval mirror above the dressing table, shaking loose her braids and brushing out her hair into a dark cloud. In the drawer she found a pink satin ribbon, just the shade of the dress she had decided to wear. She tied it around her head. She really did look pretty without her braids. Feeling quite glamorous, she went downstairs, slightly awed by the thickness of the carpets and the intricate design of the wrought-iron banisters. Searching for the dining room, she blundered into a large kitchen where a fat cook stood frying eggs at a stove. She was talking over her shoulder at the wispy maid Janna remembered from the day before. When Janna entered, she stopped and turned. Her mouth fell open, the frying pan sagged in her hand. Suddenly she pulled herself together, leveled eyebrows as dark and thick as crowbars at Janna, and rasped in a deep voice, "What are you doing here?" It sounded like German and Janna understood.

"Please," she asked, "where is the dining room?" The little maid hastily put down a boot she was cleaning and wiped her hands on her apron.

"I'll show you," she said in school German. She opened the kitchen door and pointed to the door just opposite, across the passage. She looked scared. Janna smiled reassuringly and the girl smiled back, a wavering smile of great sweetness.

As Janna entered the dining room, she saw her father and mother sitting at the table, which was surprisingly laid for six people. This room looked different too in the daylight. There were strong, bright pictures of sunflowers and corn fields on the paneled walls. Here too, French windows opened into the garden. The snow outside cast a bluish light into the room. A carved wall clock with a picture on it and long weights hanging down seemed to scrape its throat and then chimed nine times. On the table was a lavish breakfast of eggs, toast, hot milk, and steaming coffee.

Herr Oster had disappeared behind *Die Deutsche Zeitung in den Niederlanden,* the local German newspaper. Her mother, who was sipping coffee from a translucent porcelain cup, complained, "You never talk to me. I think it's rude to read at mealtimes."

Janna's father raised his eyes above the paper. "My dear Mechtild," he said, "every evening I am either your jealous husband or your besotted lover. Can't I have the mornings off?"

Mechtild dimpled. "It is rather hard on you," she conceded, pouring more coffee.

Janna ran to her mother. "Thank you for the lovely dresses," she cried, hugging her.

"Dresses?" asked her mother, who was looking lovely in a shimmering green negligée. "The one you have on is enchanting, much better than those widow's weeds of last night. But why thank me for it? Didn't Erna look after your clothes?"

"This is one of the ones you bought me," said Janna.

"But I did not buy you any clothes," her mother said, bewildered. "I was waiting to measure you. Where did you find them?"

"In the wardrobe," said Janna. "Beautiful ones."

"Heavens!" Mechtild was upset. "That good-for-nothing Corrie! I told her to clear away everything in the drawers and closets and store it in the attic. She is a lazy girl, and if I scold her, she'll say she didn't understand... though she knows German well enough. Take the dress off at once; it doesn't belong to us."

Janna's father peered over his paper. "What's the trouble, Mechtild?" he asked.

"She's wearing one of the dresses of... of the people... who lived here before."

"The van Arkels, you mean," said her husband. "What's the harm? Don't tell me that you swallow the house but choke at a dress? It suits Janna. Let her wear it." He dove behind his newspaper again. Janna saw that her mother was trembling. Was she angry or scared?

"What do you mean, swallow the house?" Frau Oster asked. "I only wanted a little place where I could have my daughter with me. Is that so bad?"

"I explained to you how it would be," her husband answered patiently. "I was against incurring the obligation."

"What obligation? It did not cost the Baron a thing."

"You don't know that, my dear. He may have had to do some bribing. But even if he didn't pay anything, we're still beholden to him."

"I only wanted something empty, something no one was using," Mechtild continued.

"And where would you find that, in overpopulated Holland?" her husband asked. "What in the world did you expect the Baron to do for you, perform a miracle? As it is, he almost did that. I'm enjoying this house very much. It's a lot better than living out of suitcases."

"Then why do you object to the Baron?"

"Because he is too fond of you, my dear."

"Nonsense," said Mechtild. "He sees a sister in me, someone to confide his troubles to. He has suffered a lot in the war; most of his family were killed, and he is never without pain from his shoulder wound. He is a sensitive person and I'm trying to help him."

Otto lowered his paper. "I don't doubt your intentions, my dear," he said. "I just don't share your faith in the Baron."

Janna was looking from one parent to the other. Their conversation was full of hidden meanings which she could not fathom, but one thing was clear: the house did not belong to her parents. It was a borrowed house.

"Did the furniture in my room also belong to the van Arkels?" she asked. She couldn't keep her disappointment out of her voice. The van Arkels must have a girl her age, and all the love and effort had been for her.

"Everything in the house belongs to them," said her mother. "We chose that room for you because it seemed just right." Janna stroked her dress. It felt soft, not scratchy, like her own dresses.

"I'll take it off, Mother, if you want me to."

"No, no," sighed her mother. "If your father says it's all right, you may wear it." She buttered some toast. "Here, eat your breakfast, my dear. Perhaps I am foolish. By the time the van Arkels get back their house, the girl may have outgrown her clothes."

Corrie, the little maid, came in with the mail and put it beside Herr Oster's plate. Herr Oster looked up at her. When she had gone, he said, "Do the servants get enough to eat?"

"Of course," said his wife. "What do you take me for?"

"Corrie looks thinner every day," he said, opening his mail.

Janna's parents began to read their letters. Janna took another slice of toast and spread it with fried egg. She was thinking about the Dutch girl who had had her room and must be exactly her size. What had she looked like and what had happened to her? Had she anything to wear now? Why had she left all her clothes and possessions behind, even her doll?

Herr Oster looked up from the letter he was reading. "Mechtild, have you seen a Rembrandt anywhere?" he asked.

"A Rembrandt!" His wife jerked to attention, her eyes widening. "Do they have a *Rembrandt* here? A genuine one? I know they're collectors—these are real Van Goghs in the dining room and there are good Impressionists in the long room—but a *Rembrandt!* No, I haven't seen it. I would have been sure to tell you if I had."

"I have a letter here from Seyss-Inquart, inquiring about it. Apparently Hitler is interested in it. He wants it for his new museum in Linz."

"We can't give it to him, it doesn't belong to us..." protested his wife, sounding frightened.

"It has nothing to do with us," said Otto. "This house belongs to the Reich now. War spoils, my dear. All we are asked to do is to take care of the picture and hand it over to the men who will be sent to collect it."

"I hate that," said his wife, covering her face with her hands.

"You'd hate it still more if you lost it and had to pay for it," said her husband. "It must be worth well over a million marks."

Frau Oster lowered her hands and looked at Otto in alarm. "What kind of picture is it?" she asked.

"It's a small picture of a church interior... the Presentation or Circumcision or something. Probably lots of shadows with a glittering gold spot in the middle... You've seen Rembrandts before. Do look for it. We should put it safely away."

"If it hasn't already been stolen," said Mechtild.

"It would be hard to get rid of," her husband assured her. "No ordinary thief would touch it."

At this moment the door opened and a pale-eyed, stocky boy of about nine swaggered into the room, followed by a bull-necked, tough-looking gentleman with a close-cropped head and eyes like oysters. Behind him tripped and twittered a small wrenlike woman.

"Good morning, Herr Oster, *gnädige Frau*," they said, bowing and clicking their heels at Janna's parents and ignoring Janna. The boy paid no attention to anybody and went straight to his plate.

"Why aren't there currant buns?" he whined. "I want currant buns."

"Janna," Frau Oster said, "these are Herr and Frau Frosch and their son, Heinz. They have the suite on the fourth floor and share their meals with us."

"How do you do," said Janna politely, shaking hands with the Frosch couple. When she came to Heinz, he put his hands behind his back and stuck out his tongue. Janna restrained an impulse to do the same. It was beneath her dignity.

"Please forgive him," chirped his mother. "He is so shy!" Shy Heinz made a rude noise.

"Well," said Frau Oster, "I'd better go look for that picture. Excuse me." And with a graceful bow to the Frosches, she made one of her superb exits.

Janna ran after her, spoiling the effect. "Let me help you!" she cried.

As they mounted the stairs to the second floor, Janna asked, "Who are they, Mother? I didn't know there were going to be other people in the house."

"Hush!" said her mother, frowning. "Not so loud. The Baron could not get us a house to ourselves. There's a shortage, you know. The Frosches are friends of Seyss-Inquart and were already installed when we came. They have the whole fourth floor. Herr Frosch is secretary to Herr Brigadeführer Rauter, the chief of security in Amsterdam. Don't offend them, please, Janna. They could make things unpleasant for us."

"They are already making it unpleasant for us," said Janna resentfully. "What a pimple that Heinz is!"

"Don't make snap judgments, Janna. You should be glad of another child in the house."

"He is much too young for me."

"He is the age your brother would have been," sighed her mother, remembering a small coffin.

Janna quickly asked, "Who is Seyss-Inquart?"

"He is the present ruler of Holland. Didn't you know? Hitler appointed him. He is an Austrian and helped us when we annexed his country."

"And the Baron, who is he?"

"The Baron?" A warm light came into her mother's eyes. "He is General Dietrich von Schönheim, a great friend of ours, an officer in the Wehrmacht who has seen many campaigns. He was wounded in Russia and is now stationed here because he is still recuperating. You'll meet him soon, he often visits us. We owe him a lot."

They had arrived at the second floor, and Frau Oster was inspecting the pictures in the passage.

"There is another front door here," said Janna, pointing at the heavy oak door. Its fanlight was making a halo of her mother's hair.

"Yes, isn't it interesting? We had a visit from Mynheer van Tonningen, the head of the Netherlands Bank, the other day and he told us about these canal houses. Most of them have two front doors: one on street level and one on the second floor."

"How do you get in from the street then?" asked Janna.

"I forgot you arrived at night! Otherwise you would have seen the stone steps leading up to the door."

Frau Oster finished examining the mottled prints in the hall, while Janna opened the door nearest the front door and peeked into a library, where the walls were so covered with books there was no room for pictures. She followed her mother into a neighboring anteroom, furnished in French style with elegant gilt chairs and sofas. It was warmed by a Franklin stove and got its light from a window opening into a shaft and from glass doors leading into another room. Janna noticed an interesting dollhouse in the corner and would have gone to look at it, but her mother restrained her.

"That's not a toy, it's an antique," she said nervously. The paintings in this room were mostly Amsterdam street scenes by an artist called Breitner.

"Mother," said Janna, "if the Frosches were here first, why do they have the fourth floor? Why did they not take the one we have?"

"The Baron arranged it all," her mother said curtly. "The Frosches are quite comfortable... There is an extra living room on the fourth floor, which I think belonged to the...to a nursemaid...and there's a boy's room, just suited for Heinz. It's a funny thing...the fourth floor seems larger than the third..." She stood musing for a moment. Then she shook herself and mounted the few steps leading to the glass doors and opened them. Janna followed her into a long hall. It was the most beautiful room Janna had ever seen. It stretched at right angles to the other rooms and seemed to extend beyond the front width of the house.

"That's another interesting thing," Janna's mother explained. "These canal houses were built in the seventeenth century when simple merchants often became richer than the old, established Dutch families. So the burghers passed a law that social position, not money, should determine the amount of canal frontage you were allowed to have. Very important people could have a door in the middle and two or three windows on each side. The less important you were, the fewer windows you were allowed. The merchant who built this house had a low social position but a lot of money and a large family. He was only allowed one window, so he built two houses side by side, each with a door and a window. Then he cheated. At the back he used the width of both houses, which resulted in this beautiful room. He also had a double garden. The next-door house, which he sold, has only the front rooms. With five stories, that is still plenty."

Janna's mother began to look at the pictures, but Janna still gazed at the room. Such space! If only they could have had it for their Youth meetings! The light from three tall windows shone between floor-length golden draperies on a gleaming parquet floor which was covered here and there with Persian scatter rugs. Little inlaid tables supported tall Chinese vases. It was easy to see that the Dutch had ships traveling to all corners of the world! A row of lyre-backed chairs stood against the wall opposite the windows. The room was so large one hardly noticed the grand piano in the far corner. On the short side nearest her, Janna saw a marble fireplace with carvings. Above it hung a huge gold-framed mirror. The ceiling was painted with gods and goddesses floating on clouds. Several chandeliers, winking with crystal, hung down from it like huge tears. The wall opposite the fireplace was half covered by an enormous painting. The other walls held smaller ones. Janna started to look at them. They reminded her of other pictures she had seen in museums: nude ladies drying themselves or on couches, tables covered with spilled food, landscapes with cows and windmills.

"Those were probably bought quite cheaply, when the painters were young," Janna's mother said appreciatively. "They are all famous Dutch Impressionists now. This one is a Post-Impressionist, Charley Toorop. Her father was an artist too." Mechtild pointed to what Janna thought an ugly picture of some huge faces, painted in broad strokes and looking as if carved out of wood.

"I don't like it," she said.

"It's powerful," said her mother. "How do you like this one?" She was standing in front of a shimmering gray picture of an old beggar, sitting under the drooping coats of a secondhand-clothes shop, staring dreamily into the distance. Something in his face reminded Janna of the little man in the train.

"It's the sort of subject Rembrandt might have chosen," said Frau Oster. "Only handled quite differently. It's painted by a Jew: Jozef Israels."

"Do Jews paint?" asked Janna, surprised.

"They paint, they compose music, they act, they write..." her mother said gently. "They are a very gifted people."

Janna flushed. "That's not true," she said. "Whatever they do is only imitated from the Aryans; they are parasites of Aryan culture..."

"Who told you that?"

"I learned it at school. It's in *Mein Kampf,*" said Janna. Her mother was silent. "That's right, isn't it?" insisted Janna, who did not like the expression on her mother's face.

"I can't believe anyone said that about the Jews," her mother said slowly. "Whatever they may have done politically, the world is full of their creations. We owe them our Bible, and they have influenced all our modern thinking: Bergson, Karl Marx, Albert Einstein, Freud...to name only a few..."

"But it's bad, Mother," said Janna earnestly. "It's un-German."

Her mother sighed. "How like your father you are."

Janna wondered whether her mother meant it as a compliment. Her eyes had been straying toward the large picture at the end of the room. It represented a family gathered around a table, exactly in the way that Janna felt families should. They were all looking at the antics of a baby lifted in his mother's arms. A bearded father had lowered the book he was reading, two adolescent boys were glancing up from their homework, and a girl of Janna's age held out a doll. The baby, painted in quick, fresh strokes, kicked its legs and reached for it. The lamplight created a luminous circle, uniting all the figures. It slanted across the mother's face, which shone with gentle pride. Tendrils of her hair curled delicately golden against the shadows of the girl's blue velvet dress. The boys' faces were strongly lit, showing square jaws and smooth cheekbones. Their blue eyes twinkled. The father, half in shadow, looked as if his mind were still busy with what he had been reading. Something about his high forehead and firm lips seemed to promise that he was not one to pass by when others were in need. The kind of father you could run and tell your troubles to, thought Janna. But she was most interested in the girl, who was very pretty, with dark hair and eyes like her father. The others were all blond. Janna's mother noticed her interest.

"Do you admire that picture?" she asked. "It's by a young Dutch artist and only recently painted. I like it because the girl resembles you."

"Does she?" Janna blushed with pleasure. She studied the picture again. Surely she wasn't as pretty as that? She knew she wasn't. Yet there was something familiar about the picture. Janna looked closer. It was the doll! There was no mistaking that smug expression, though here the doll still had some hair straggling from the top of its head. And the velvet dress...hadn't she seen its counterpart in the wardrobe upstairs?

"Mother!" she exclaimed. "That doll...I've got it in my room. Mother, this is a picture of the van Arkels...don't you see? That's the girl whose dress I'm wearing! Now we know what they look like...isn't that marvelous!" She turned around. Her mother had grown pale. She had put her hand to her head.

"We've searched enough for today," she muttered and hurried out of the room. Janna followed her slowly. She found her mother lying on her bed upstairs.

"What's the matter, Mother?" she asked, alarmed.

"I've got one of my headaches. Get me some aspirin, dear," she said, scarcely moving her lips. "They're in the drawer of my dressing table."

"Do you mean this bottle?" asked Janna. "It's empty."

"Oh, I'd forgotten, I'm out of it. And in half an hour I'm due at rehearsal. What shall I do?" her mother moaned.

"I'll go and get you some," said Janna.

"Alone? Do you dare? That would be wonderful, darling. It's quite close. You'll find money in my handbag over there on the chair. Take a gulden. When you go out, follow the canal to the left till you come to a bridge. There's a cross street there with shops. The druggist is on the corner. Please hurry, and thanks! You're an angel."

Janna was glad of the opportunity to put on the lovely blue coat trimmed with white fur which she had seen in the wardrobe. It had a little cap to match. She let herself out by the top front door so that she could try the steps. They were slippery with melting snow; she had to hold on to the iron railing. Reaching the cobbled street, she looked around curiously, inhaling the peculiar canal smell. Though the snow was mostly gone from the street, the stepped gables of the houses opposite were still trimmed in white. The water of the canal murkily reflected the houses and trees opposite. Little wisps of straw and leaves bobbed among fragments of ice on its dark surface. Janna heard the clatter of wooden shoes behind her. She looked around. Some children started to wave at her, then stopped...and ran. The click-clack of their shoes echoed from the houses.

"Nella—Nella van Arkel..." shrieked a voice. "Have you come back? Did the Muffs give you back your house?" Janna turned around. The girl who had called to her stood still, stopping in her tracks when she saw Janna's face. She gave an exclamation of disgust and gave Janna a hostile look. Then she jerked around and ran back to her house, which was next to Janna's. She was one of the children Janna had seen playing in the garden that morning. Though she had spoken in Dutch, Janna understood. The girl had mistaken her for the van Arkel girl, whose name was Nella.

When Janna arrived at the bridge, it was not hard to find the druggist. There was little traffic; only Germans seemed to own cars. One passed, filled with singing Wehrmacht soldiers.

There were people in the druggist's shop, which had a counter crowded with glass jars and a brass weighing scale. The customers stopped talking as Janna entered. They all stared at her, then averted their eyes. An old lady had just bought something and was snapping her bag shut. She gave a start of surprise when she saw Janna and began to smile. Then her face froze and her eyes narrowed. There was a hush in the shop as the lady stood staring at Janna, her cheeks slowly flushing. Then her lips tightened, her eyes sparkled, and before Janna knew what was happening, the old lady had darted at her and given her a resounding smack in the face. With a strangled exclamation she then turned and hurried out of the shop.

Janna stood dumbfounded. Her cheek tingled. She could not believe what had happened. There was a general sigh as the other people in the shop let go of their breath. Somewhere a clock chimed.

The lady behind the counter bent forward and addressed Janna in German. "What can I do for the Fräulein?" Then she added, "That old lady...she thought she saw a friend's child; she was disappointed... Please forgive her."

Janna asked for aspirin. Everybody began to talk again.

When Janna walked home with her purchase, she grew more and more angry. That lady would not have dared slap her if she'd been a grownup. People thought you could do anything to a child. It was unfair! This was a beastly city, a cold, horrid, nasty city. Her father was right. The Dutch were awful.

When she had given her mother the medicine and the change, she went to her room and took off Nella's clothes. Returning them to the wardrobe, she vowed never to wear them again.

A Fountain in the Garden

JANNA HAD FOUND SOME NOTEPAPER in the desk in her room and was writing to Hildegarde. There was so much she wanted to say, but all she managed to get down was:

Dear Hildegarde,
How are you all? It was so sad to leave you. The book is lovely. I've finished it but I'm starting all over again. It is horrid here. The house is beautiful but the Dutch people are unfriendly. The German child who lives in the house is only nine. I am homesick for the Black Forest. There are no mountains here and people act as if they thought Germans were bad. How is the play going? Who is acting Brunhilde, Ilse or Marianne? I wish I were there.
Your loving Janna

She licked the envelope shut and looked for a stamp. When she did not find any inside the desk, she opened the drawers below and found some of Nella's schoolbooks. She spent some time comparing Nella's marks with her own. The Dutch children were ahead, but they probably didn't have to work on farms every afternoon. Nella was better at drawing, but she didn't have as good marks for composition. You could see that Nella had been fond of drawing. All her copybooks were illustrated with sketches. Funny little figures danced between her sums, and garlands of flowers surrounded her grammar. Dutch teachers must be more lenient than German ones. Then Janna got a shock. On a loose piece of paper she found a caricature of Hitler. He was unmistakable with his small mustache and dark cowlick. He was trampling, with big boots over a lot of small houses with Dutch gables. From his hands dropped bombs, and a balloon out of his mouth said in Gothic letters the German words, "I want peace."

Janna sat still as a stone. She had begun to think of Nella as a friend, but to make fun of *Hitler* was sacrilege.

"What have you got there?" asked Heinz's voice near her elbow. Janna almost dropped the drawing. She quickly pushed it back into the drawer.

"Nothing," she said. Then, angrily, "What are you doing in my room?"

"I want you to come and play with me," said Heinz. "There's a recreation room and a big garden with a swing and a summerhouse. Wait till I show you."

"All right," said Janna. At least Heinz was German, if he had nothing else to his credit. "But next time, knock on the door," she added.

Heinz began to talk excitedly, pointing out things as if they belonged to him, a trait that irritated Janna.

"My father says to be careful of those statues in the hall. They're valuable. Most everything in this house is valuable. When I'm grown up, I'm not going to have a single valuable thing in my house. Don't go into the kitchen, the maids are mean. Corrie shoved a broom into my face. My mother says if she does it again my father will fire her."

"And what did you do?" asked Janna.

"Oh, I can't remember..." said Heinz. "I probably left my soldiers lying around. She hates my soldiers because they are our Wehrmacht and SS. She threw some out the other day. I found them in the trash can. Look, that's the recreation room, it's got a real billiard table and lots of games. But I want to show you the garden first."

"Let's get our coats then," said Janna, fetching her school coat out of the hall closet.

When they entered the garden, Janna was glad she had come. It was a beautiful place, surrounded by an ivy-covered fence. There were old apple trees in the back. One held a swing on an outstretched limb. Heinz ran to it. Janna's attention was caught by a pretty little fountain standing among what later would probably be flowerbeds. It was made of marble with a round, wide basin. In the middle three mermaids danced, their tails touching, their arms swinging open like flower petals. Water must have gushed between them in the summer, falling over dainty heads and shoulders. Now they were covered with snow.

Poor things, thought Janna, climbing on the brim of the basin and starting to brush away the snow. It was fun to see the lovely little faces appear, laughing up at her as if thanking her. She scooped some snow out of a hollow and saw something glitter. She picked it up and gazed at it. It was a little ring.

Janna tried it on. It fit. Perhaps it was Nella's. Perhaps she'd been playing in the fountain and lost it… Janna had always wanted a ring…

She looked up at the mermaids, who smiled down at her. It's their present, thought Janna. I'm going to keep it. She felt a little guilty. Her mother had said… but that was *inside* the house. How could anyone be sure this ring belonged to Nella?

"What are you doing there, Janna? Come on…" Heinz cried imperiously. He was sitting on the swing. "Come and push me!" But Janna was admiring her ring and did not push very hard.

"Just like a girl," said Heinz scornfully, jumping off and running to the summerhouse. It was overgrown with ivy; an unpleasant, dank place with drifts of snow in the corners and on the metal chairs. Heinz cleaned a chair for her and gallantly offered it, but when she sat down, he jerked it away so that she landed on the cold, wet ground.

"Horrible boy!" she cried, slapping the snow from her skirt. "If you behave like that I won't stay," and she marched off.

"Please come back," Heinz called after her. "I promise I won't play tricks any more." Janna wavered. She did not like Heinz, but there was nobody else.

"If you come back I'll show you a secret," said Heinz.

"All right," said Janna, retracing her steps. "What secret?"

Heinz walked to the fence which separated the van Arkel property from the one next door where Janna had seen the children playing. He pulled back strands of ivy and revealed a clever hideaway where an old chair wobbled on a bit of carpet, which was sodden with melting snow.

"Look through the peephole," he said. There was a large knothole in the wood of the fence. When you sat on the chair, you could see through it with one eye. Janna noticed that the snowman was melting. The hat sagged, the carrot had fallen off. There were no children in the garden.

"I don't see anything," she said.

"Of course not. They always go in when I come out. But when I sit here a long time and keep quiet, they think I'm gone and then I can spy on them," said Heinz with satisfaction.

"And what's the fun of that?"

"Fun? It isn't *fun*," said Heinz indignantly. "It's work. I'm helping our war. Don't you know we're fighting a war?"

"We're fighting the Russians and the English and the Americans," said Janna, "not the Dutch. They're part of Germany now."

"That's what you think. We're fighting them all the time. You should hear my father! This country's supposed to be called Westland now, not the Netherlands, and the Dutch are supposed to obey Hitler; but they don't want to belong to us. They still want their old queen."

"How do you know?"

"By the things they do. They don't give to our Winterhelp. They pretend to, but the collection box is always full of buttons and pebbles and bits of glass. They're supposed to give up their bicycles, but they only give us the old ones and they keep the new ones hidden somewhere. They print secret newspapers with pictures of the queen and the princesses, and they listen to Radio Orange from London, and then they do what the queen tells them. If I hear the people next door doing that, I'll tell my father and they'll all be put into prison."

"How horrid," said Janna.

"Why? The Dutch are our enemies; they're dangerous, don't you know? It's not safe here for Germans. My father won't let me go out alone on the street, I might be pushed into a canal. Don't you know how the Dutch hate us?"

"Maybe we would hate the Dutch," said Janna slowly, "if they came into *our* country and gave it a different name and told us what to do..."

"What a silly thing to say," said Heinz scornfully. "They're not strong enough. This is much too small a country."

Janna was looking at the back of the house, all covered over with ivy. She remembered what her mother had told her.

"Who lives in the garden on the other side?" she said.

"Only grownups," said Heinz. "They don't even have a dog. They never go outside."

"And who lives in the house next door in front, the one without a garden?"

"Two old ladies," said Heinz. "Haven't you seen them? They're always sitting in their window and looking into the little mirrors on each side. I bet they spy on us. My father says when people get that old they should be put to sleep." A shiver went down Janna's back as she remembered Aunt Hedwig. She turned and almost ran into the house. It was no use trying to be friends with Heinz, she thought. When she passed the kitchen, a lovely smell made her peep inside. There was no one there, but a rich soup was bubbling on the stove and nine pink meatballs sat on a plate waiting to be fried. Janna withdrew and went upstairs. Nine meatballs for eight people. They might be expecting company.

As she arrived at the second floor, she saw that Corrie was admitting someone at the front door. It was a German officer in uniform. Corrie offered to take his coat, but the officer said he had only come to deliver a note and would leave right away.

"The *gnädige Frau* isn't in," said Corrie in her best German. "Only Frau Frosch and Fräulein Janna."

"Ah, Fräulein Janna! Tell her I'd like to meet her," the officer said in an agreeable cultured voice. Corrie showed him into the anteroom.

Janna hadn't waited. The glimpse she had caught of the officer, who seemed to have a very high rank, had been exciting. She ran to her room and changed quickly into Nella's blue velvet dress. It was only a few hours since she had vowed never to wear Nella's clothes again, but then she had not known that a handsome officer was going to call. She washed her face and hands and brushed her hair till it was glossy. By the time Corrie found her, she was ready.

The officer was standing over the Franklin stove, warming his hands. He had opened his greatcoat and laid his cap and gloves on the table. He was tall, with a long, mobile face, a high forehead, and deep-set, rather melancholy eyes. His dark-blond hair was swept back smoothly. He turned to Janna, and when his eyes met hers, mysterious and probing, she felt herself blush.

"So this is the daughter?" he said pleasantly. "We've waited for you a long time, your mother and I." He smiled as if he approved of her, but it did not lighten the shadow in his eyes.

Janna frowned. What right had he to wait for her, and why had he not mentioned her father? Summoning all her dignity, she said, "I am Johanna Oster. Who are you?"

The officer responded immediately. He stood erect, clicked his heels, and bowed. "I beg your pardon," he said. "Let me introduce myself. My name is Dietrich von Schönheim."

"The Baron," said Janna, looking up at him wonderingly.

"Yes," said the officer. "The Baron." Janna again felt his gaze on her. She wanted to shake it off. Motioning to a chair, she sat down herself.

"Do you like living in Amsterdam?" she asked politely, folding her hands in her lap. The Baron had taken the chair. He looked at her and burst out laughing.

"How like your mother you are!" he exclaimed.

"Everyone says I'm like my father," said Janna stiffly.

"In looks, yes," agreed the Baron. "But in manner...you're the image of her."

"Do you know my mother well?" Janna asked coldly.

"We are dear friends," the Baron answered. "We're like brother and sister." A quick glance convinced Janna that she had better look away. The Baron's face was too flatteringly attentive. She stared down at her hands and noticed for the first time that her fingers were lacing and unlacing, just the way her mother's did when she was agitated. It was a disconcerting discovery. She put her hands at her sides and cleared her throat.

"Can I offer you something?" she asked. "Are you thirsty?"

The Baron laughed again. He stretched out his hands and captured one of Janna's between them. They were large and warm. "Can't we be friends?" he pleaded.

Janna's heart longed to say yes, but something made her answer sternly, "I don't know you well enough."

The Baron withdrew his hands. "Of course you don't," he said. Then he went on lightly, "Would you like to be an actress when you grow up?"

"Oh yes," she said eagerly. "I was going to be Brunhilde in a play, only then I had to leave."

"So you know the story of the *Nibelungen*?" the Baron asked thoughtfully. He had stood up and was looking down on her. Janna glimpsed an array of decorations on his uniform.

"Your parents are acting in a modern version of the story of Sieglinde," he went on. "Would you like to see it?"

Janna jumped from her chair. "I'd love to...could I?" she asked.

"I'll take you," promised the Baron, picking up his gloves and cap.

"Now I have to go. But remember, we have a date!" He kissed Janna's hand, the one with the ring. Janna watched him go and stared after him, her feelings in a muddle.

There were meatballs for lunch that day but no visitor.

The Play

Janna had never had any jewelry, she certainly had never owned anything that was real gold. She wondered why people talked about the gold of wheat or of sunflowers. People were always using the word "gold" when they meant yellow. Gold wasn't a color, it was a shine. She thought all this while studying the ring. The fact that it didn't belong to her, that it must be part of the van Arkel possessions, nagged at the back of her mind, but she wasn't paying attention to it. She was getting very fond of the little ring. It somehow made her feel grownup, less of a schoolgirl.

The Baron was as good as his word. One morning Janna was sitting at breakfast with her parents, after the Frosches had left, when a written invitation arrived for her to see the play *Sieglinde*. Her mother, noticing the crest on the envelope, was going to open it when she saw it was addressed to Fräulein Johanna Oster. Janna flushed with pleasure, opened it, and showed the invitation to her mother.

"I forgot," said Mechtild. "You did meet the Baron, didn't you? He told me. Isn't that kind of him!"

"Do you think the play is suitable for a child?" asked her husband.

"I know it already," Janna blurted out. "It's about Siegmund and Sieglinde. They were twins but they were separated as babies, and later when they were grownup they met and fell in love. Sieglinde was married already, so they ran away, but her husband killed Siegmund, and later Sieglinde died too, though Brunhilde tried to save her."

"You see, Otto," said her mother. "It's no use trying to shield Janna from the facts of the story. She knows them already. It's only fair that she should see her parents act." She looked at her daughter and said suddenly, "Where did you get that ring, Janna?"

"I...I found it..." Janna stammered.

"In the house? I told you...everything is..."

"Outside," said Janna quickly.

"Let me see...is it valuable? Otto, have a look..."

"I can't tell," said Otto, turning the little ring between his blunt fingers. "It could be gold, but I see no hallmark...It might be brass. Does it make your finger green, Janna?"

"No," said Janna.

"Then it may be gold-plated. For goodness' sake, Mechtild, don't make a fuss about a trinket. Let the child keep it." Janna breathed a sigh of relief.

The Baron did things in style. He fetched her in his Mercedes. Janna wore the velvet dress and the pretty coat and cap. She could not disgrace the Baron by going in her school clothes.

"You look very nice," he praised, and she blushed. His eyes seemed to probe into her most secret thoughts. The chauffeur opened the door of the car and they soon sat side by side and were driven through the dark streets. There was no mist this time. Moonlight silvered the edges of the buildings and shone milkily into the canals. Janna looked at the Baron. His face was shadowy, but as he smiled at her she could see the gleam of his teeth.

"So you know the whole story of the Ring," he said.

Janna nodded. "We had to learn it at school. It's Hitler's favorite story."

"So I believe," said the Baron dryly. "Do you understand the meaning of it?"

"I think I do," said Janna. "They explained it to us." She thought for a moment. She did not want to make a bad impression. "It's about greed," she said. "Greed for gold, like the democracies have. The dwarfs start it by making the ring, and even Wotan gets greedy and plays tricks to get it. Siegfried is the hero and he gives the ring away because he is too noble to be greedy, and Brunhilde only wants it because it's Siegfried's pledge of love, but the curse slays them all the same...though even in death they are greater than the greedy dwarfs who triumph over them."

"Very interesting," murmured the Baron. "Have you ever seen the operas?"

"Oh no, Erna could not afford it, and before, in Berlin, I was too young."

"That's a pity. The music says so much more than the words. I think the main idea of the story is that there is a curse on stolen power. There is a legitimate power which goes with responsibility and discipline. To want absolute power is to court disaster, for it is only an illusion. In the *Nibelungen* the gods who grasp at it go up in flames. Yet at the end the music of the opera tells us that after their destruction a new order will arise where power will come only through love. This is shown in *Parsifal*. There the self-sacrifice of the knights overcomes the evil machinations of the sorcerer. It's the last of the Ring series, though it is not generally included. It was also Wagner's last work."

"I did not know there was another one," said Janna, immensely flattered at being addressed as an equal.

"Someday, if we have a chance, we'll go to see *Parsifal*," the Baron promised. "In the play I'm taking you to, Siegmund and Sieglinde are ordinary people in modern dress. Siegmund is drafted and dies in battle. Sieglinde dies in childbirth. Brunhilde doesn't come into it. It's a dreary play, but your mother makes it great."

The car stopped suddenly. There were beams of flashlights and shadowy men in uniform.

"What's the matter, Ludwig?" the Baron asked.

"The SS are arresting somebody, Herr General..." answered the chauffeur.

"I'll have a look." The Baron left the car and Janna followed. She didn't want to miss this. The SS were holding a lanky, skinny lad who was convulsively clutching a paper bag. He gaped like a fish; his Adam's apple bobbed up and down.

"I don't understand..." he quavered. His voice ended in a squeak.

"You're the right age, you should have reported for labor. You'll have to come with us," the SS officer told him.

"No, no, I'm only sixteen and my mother is ill, she has nobody else..." the boy said desperately. "I only went out to get her medicine..."

"What's this?" asked the Baron, shouldering aside the SS officers, who stood to attention at once when their flashlights revealed the Baron's high rank.

"What do you think we run in Germany, a kindergarten?" the Baron asked. "Even if this boy were the right age, what sort of labor could he do to justify the cost of his transportation? Let him go back to his mother, for heaven's sake!"

"We have orders," said the SS men.

"I take the responsibility," the Baron answered firmly. The lad, finding himself free, scurried off like a rabbit, and the Baron returned to his car, after showing Janna in first.

"Sadistic idiots," he muttered between his teeth. He seemed very angry. Janna was impressed. The Baron, she thought, had legitimate power.

They stopped in front of the dark theater and entered the building along with a lot of other people who were all speaking German. The Baron was very popular with the ladies. Many approached him, started to talk to him. He was polite, exchanged pleasantries, but never made Janna feel he had forgotten her. His hand was at her back, gently pushing her toward her seat. He bought a program for her. It had a photograph on it of her father and mother. Janna gazed around, enchanted. She had never seen so many beautifully dressed people.

The play was strange. Janna hardly recognized the story in all the ordinary everyday chatter and the plain clothes. Perhaps, if it had kept to its romantic setting, she would not have found it so disturbing to watch her parents on the stage. They made it all so real! Her father was Sieglinde's husband, Hunding, and he was perfectly horrid. Janna tried to remember that it was only a play, but her father was too good an actor, she kept forgetting. In this play Siegmund and Sieglinde did not know they were twins till it was too late. Janna's mother was beautiful. Her voice and gestures compelled you to look at her. You hardly noticed the pale blond actor who played Siegmund.

There were moments when Janna sat on the edge of her seat and held her breath. She wasn't the only one; the audience was visibly moved by the plight of the ill-starred lovers. The sleeping tablets had been put into Hunding's drink and the twins had had their talk and were sneaking out of the house. The first act was over. The curtain fell to thunderous applause. The lights went on and Janna glanced at her escort. He sat in a dream, his arms folded, his eyes staring unseeing into the distance, his lips firmly closed.

"Did you not like it either?" she asked. She had to repeat her question before he shook himself awake and looked at her.

"Didn't you like it?" he asked. His voice was a little hoarse. "It's a poor play, but the acting..."

"It's seeing my father and mother like that...as if it were *real*..." stammered Janna. "It...it frightened me...Father was so horrid!" She found instantaneous understanding.

"Come backstage," the Baron said. "Then you'll see it wasn't real." She followed him through narrow passages where people greeted the Baron as if he were a familiar figure, to the dressing room, where her father and mother were preparing themselves for the next act. Her father frowned at first but relaxed when he saw Janna.

"She got frightened," explained the Baron. "You acted too well, Otto."

Otto looked pleased. "I'm still your old papa," he said, grinning. "But remember, I've got to make people believe that your mother has a reason to go running off with that pale apology of a Siegmund." It made Janna laugh.

The Baron had been whispering something to Janna's mother that was making her blush. Bells rang, and the Baron and Janna went back to their seats.

The rest of the play was less harrowing to Janna because it seemed less real. All the same, her mother looked so frail and deserted and died so beautifully that Janna found the tears streaming down her cheeks when the lights went on again.

The Baron wiped them off with his handkerchief. "I can see you're not used to plays," he said, which was unfair, for his own eyes shone suspiciously.

The curtain went up and down many times while people clapped. Janna's mother got a bouquet of orchids. "She gets them every night," someone whispered behind Janna. "I wonder who sends them…"

People were moving toward the exits.

"It's no use going backstage," the Baron told Janna as he propelled her along with his hand. "There'll be a mob there, wanting autographs. Silly custom," he added. "We'll wait in the car for them."

The chauffeur opened the door. It was cold in the car and the Baron wrapped a rug around Janna. He had scarcely settled the folds when the drone of planes overhead disturbed the quiet and antiaircraft guns began to spit fire. Searchlights crisscrossed the sky; there was a deafening burst of explosives. Janna disappeared under the rug, trembling, but she felt the Baron's steady hand on her shoulder as his voice said, "Don't worry, they're after definite targets in Germany—this is not a dangerous area."

Janna's head emerged again. "But Cologne then, and Mainz?" she quavered.

"Those were enemy towns to them," the Baron said. "They are trying to spare Dutch civilians."

"Oh." Janna sat straight again. The noise did not last long, the airplanes went on, the sky became dark again.

"How can you be a soldier?" Janna asked with a shudder.

The Baron fumbled for a cigarette and lit it. "There is a need for soldiers as well as policemen, as long as all men are not of good will," he said. "But I agree that it is often unpleasant. I had no choice. It was all my brothers and I were fit for. We were raised in a castle in Bavaria, we were noblemen, and it was understood that noblemen don't learn useful crafts. All they are supposed to do is fight. We could ride horses when we were five, and our bodies were trained and drilled till they were perfect. We learned to obey and not to flinch at pain. We were also taught history and literature and music... oh, we were happy enough. Above all, we were taught '*noblesse oblige*,' the duty of being kind to the helpless. My father was a devout Catholic. He died of a broken heart."

"Why?" asked Janna.

"Because my three brothers were killed in battle... but most of all because he disagreed with Hitler about why and how a war should be fought. Never mind, we won't go into that now. You're coughing. Does my cigarette bother you? Sorry." The Baron opened the window and threw it out.

"Will my parents come soon?" asked Janna.

"As soon as they've got rid of the autograph hunters."

"If you weren't here, how would they get home?" asked Janna. She was looking out of the window.

"On the tram, or they'd walk," said the Baron. "It isn't far."

"Heinz says the streets aren't safe for Germans," Janna remarked.

The Baron gave a short laugh. "A lot safer than they are for the Dutch," he said. "We are the only ones who are armed. Curious thing, this fear of the conqueror for the conquered."

"There they are," said Janna, catching sight of her parents.

Not much was said when they drove home. As they reached the house, the Baron took his leave. "Thank you for a lovely evening," said Janna, stretching out her hand. He bent over and kissed it, just as he had done to her mother.

"Are we friends now?" he asked, his eyes dark in his face. Janna withdrew her hand.

"Maybe," she said. She really did like him.

The Baron turned to her mother. He laughed. "You all over, Mechtild," he said, and jumped into the car.

A Tea Party

JANNA SAT IN FRONT OF THE MIRROR, admiring her ring. When she moved her hand, it flashed. She had compared it with the ring in her *Nibelungen* book and they were alike, plain gold rings. The *Nibelungen* ring was magic: perhaps this one was too, perhaps it would bring her luck. She breathed on her ring and rubbed it. When Aladdin rubbed his lamp, a genie came out, but a genie could not come out of a ring.

She was feeling lonely. Her parents were away so often. Every night they were at the theater and they had rehearsals during the day. Even when she was home Mechtild seldom had time for Janna, what with her dressmakers and hairdressers. Janna missed her Youth meetings. She had no friends, for you could not count Heinz. And the people in the house were all so strange. Frau Frosch seemed to live in a world of her own, from which she emerged occasionally to utter absurdities. Herr Frosch was like a dark cloud with a grumble. He seemed to have a secret magic, a black magic, Janna thought. She avoided him.

Mina was like the Norns in her book, always uttering prophecies. She'd appear when you least expected her. Sometimes she disappeared into thin air. Once Janna saw her go into the long room. She followed from a distance, curious to know what Mina wanted there. But when she entered the room, there was no trace of Mina. Janna searched everywhere, behind the drapes and the Chinese screen, even under the piano. There was no other door and the windows were too far above the ground. Janna finally gave up, half convinced that she had only imagined seeing Mina go in there. As for making friends with her, you might as well try to make friends with a crocodile.

Corrie was much more approachable. She laughed at Janna's attempts to speak Dutch and corrected her pronunciation. She didn't mind chattering in her own language, giving Janna a chance to learn it. Janna noticed its similarity to Low German, which she used to speak with her Westphalian grandmother. But Corrie was always tired. Janna wondered whether she was ill. One day, at dinner, Corrie came in with a heavy tureen of soup. She staggered all of a sudden, dropped the tureen, clasped her head, and sagged to the floor. Herr Oster carried her to the sofa in the corner. Frau Oster chafed her wrists. Janna ran to fetch Mina, while Herr Frosch lamented over the soup. Mina brought ammonia and a rag. Corrie was lying back, white and still. Janna feared she was dead. Mina held the drenched rag under Corrie's nose. Her eyelids fluttered and opened.

"What happened?" she asked weakly.

"You fainted," said Mina.

"She doesn't weigh more than a ten-year-old," said Otto. "Does she eat enough?"

"Do you, Corrie?" asked Mina. "You've been eating your meals while I was out of the kitchen. Have you been starving yourself?"

Corrie seemed frightened, her round blue eyes opened wide. "I only took what you gave me...nothing else..." she quavered. "They're all depending on me to bring them something..."

"She's been taking her meals home to her family," Mina told Frau Oster. "She has her parents and five younger sisters."

"For goodness' sake," exclaimed Frau Oster, appalled. "Why didn't she take some extra food and eat her own?"

"She'd consider that stealing," said Mina primly.

"Well, I give her permission," said Frau Oster. "And you too, Mina, if you have starving relatives somewhere. The idea! Poor Corrie...is her father out of work?"

"No, he has a good job, *gnädige Frau*," said Mina tolerantly. "But money does not mean anything; there just isn't enough food to go around." Frau Oster blushed. Meanwhile, Janna had been wondering whether to test her ring. Rubbing it a little, she wished Corrie to get better.

But Herr Oster, who had fetched a glass of wine and made Corrie drink it, took all the credit when she revived.

"When are we having dinner?" complained Herr Frosch. Mina and Janna cleared away the mess and then Mina brought in fresh soup.

From that day on, Mina packed a basket of food for Corrie to take home every evening. It was a pleasure to see her fill out and regain color in her cheeks. Soon the house echoed with her singing as she scrubbed the floors.

> *"My father is a jolly man,*
> *He thinks the world of me.*
> *He only works for the fun of it,*
> *And I'm the same as he."*

"What kind of a song is that?" asked Janna.

"It's a soldier's song," said Corrie.

"Our soldiers sing of bravery and victory," said Janna.

"I know," said Corrie. "I've heard them. I'm glad ours don't. War is nothing to boast about."

Janna had got interested in Corrie's family and encouraged her to talk about them.

"They're so happy with the food I bring home," Corrie said.

"Of course, they aren't selfish about it, they share with the neighbors. Only I'm worried carrying that basket. There are so many people who'd think nothing of doing you in for a basket of food. The Mussert boys are the worst, those nasty Dutch traitors... They'd kill you for the fun of it. They're lording it over us now, and they've stolen our old prince's flag—orange, white, and blue—so we can't use it any more. They're allowed to parade it around, while we can't hang out our national flag without being clapped into prison. What's worse, they've stolen our old rallying cry, 'Hou zee,' which means 'Stick to the sea.' It's used instead of 'Hurrah,' but they've made a traitor word of it, the scoundrels"—suddenly Corrie clapped her hand to her mouth—"There I go again!" she cried. "It's my month to speak kindly and look what I've been saying."

"What do you mean, your month to speak kindly?" asked Janna.

"Well, you see," said Corrie, embarrassed, "this priest has started the League without a Name; anyone can belong to it. Once a bunch of Mussert men came to our meeting to start trouble. They sat in the back with their belts and big boots. But Father preached so beautifully on love of your neighbor that even the Mussert men cried. Father says we must reform ourselves before we can improve the world. Every month he sends out a leaflet with a special task for us. Last month we weren't allowed to speak or listen to scandal. This month it's kind words. You don't know how wicked you are till you try to be good."

"I don't think you're wicked," said Janna. She had been impressed with Corrie's self-sacrifice and honesty.

"I don't mean to be, and that's for sure," said Corrie. "It just comes natural."

The van Arkel family had captured Janna's fancy. At night, before she went to sleep, she imagined she was Nella's twin sister and they had all sorts of adventures. Nella was always getting into trouble and then Janna had to help her out. That was easy, because she had the ring. When she rubbed it, her wishes came true, and that way she could extricate Nella from all sorts of hopeless situations. Afterward Nella's parents thanked her with tears in their eyes.

She often stood in front of the big picture, studying it. She had invented names for the boys. It irritated her that whoever did the cleaning, probably Corrie, often left the picture hanging crooked. She had to keep straightening it.

She explored the rest of the house. The recreation room was Heinz's domain. There he massed his tin soldiers on the billiard table and held battles with cannons and paper airplanes, when he wasn't sitting in his spy hole or shooting birds with his popgun. He was always trying to get Janna to play backgammon or checkers with him, but he was such a bad loser that Janna thought it no fun.

She liked to play with the dollhouse in the anteroom. Its front was like that of a canal house with a sawtoothed gable. Inside, the rooms were full of old-fashioned furniture: canopied beds, a tiny spinning wheel, a coal range, a milk churner, warming pans, etc. China dolls in period costumes leaned stiffly against the chairs.

Janna also liked rummaging in the table drawers, discovering lace gloves, a magnifying glass, ballet slippers, pencils, and feathered fans. Janna's mother would stop her when she noticed it.

"Janna, remember, nothing is ours..." She said it all the time, whether Janna was winding up an old music box or leafing through photograph albums. "Take care, don't touch, leave it alone..." It got to be tiresome. Mina was worse. Janna could not peek into a room, open a closet, or investigate a cubbyhole without Mina suddenly appearing like a spider in a web, saying, "Take care, Little Miss Snoop, that your nose doesn't get caught in a door!"

Janna was glad when her parents found a teacher for her. He was a

Dutch law student who needed extra money. "We tried to find a German tutor for you," her father explained. "But they're scarce. This Dutchman is all right. He is excused from labor in Germany because of his poor health. His friends call him Erasmus, after the Dutch philosopher of the sixteenth century. They say he is brilliant. Heinz's father wants him to teach Heinz too, so you won't be alone."

The library was arranged suitably with tables and chairs. When Hugo van Hoorn entered the room that first morning, Janna felt embarrassed. He was short and one shoulder was higher than the other. He had a pronounced hump on his back. He looked frail.

"He is a hunchback," whispered Heinz.

But when Hugo sat down and began to talk, Janna forgot his handicap. His face came alive and proved quite attractive. His brown eyes, under his domed forehead, smiled at her behind flickering glasses. They shone with intelligence and understanding. Janna's pity and concern soon changed into admiration. She realized that she had never had a better teacher.

But that first day was awkward because of Heinz. He showed no respect, answered Hugo's questions rudely, and imitated the teacher's posture and gestures behind his back. Janna did not want to look, but Heinz knew how to draw her attention and she had to laugh, whether she wanted to or not. After a little of this, Hugo turned around and beckoned Heinz to face him.

"Let me enjoy it too," he said quietly. It wasn't funny, with Hugo looking on, but Hugo smiled serenely and said, "Very good, young man. Now let's see if you can do as well in arithmetic."

Heinz soon found out that he did not meet Hugo's standards for his age. That irritated him; he began to play tricks, disappearing under the table and tickling Janna's legs. He shook the table when Janna had to write and let a beetle dipped in ink crawl all over her books.

Janna complained to her parents. "With him there I'll never learn anything," she said. So Heinz was withdrawn from the lessons. His mother undertook his education and could be heard every morning running through the house calling, "Heinz, Heinzchen, time for your lessons!" while the wretched boy hid somewhere. Janna thought him a spoiled brat. She slept under his bedroom and could hear his tantrums almost every night. She wondered how his parents put up with it.

She got to love her lessons with Hugo. Under his gentle direction many mysteries which had baffled her in mathematics were explained. Ancient history came alive. German literature acquired new glamour. She read poets she had never heard of: Heine and Rilke. At her request, Hugo taught her Dutch too.

Janna was much happier now, with work to do and interesting things to think about. Herr Frosch was the only fly in her ointment. She did not like him. He talked rudely to his wife, was barely polite to Janna's mother, and shouted at Corrie. The only one he treated with some respect was Janna's father. The two men often agreed on political issues. But Mechtild wasn't finished complaining about Herr Frosch.

"Otto, it's ridiculous. He does what he likes without telling me. Either I run this household or I don't. Let his wife do it. Maybe she can manage him."

"Frau Frosch?" Otto chuckled. "We'd be in the soup. You'll just have to put up with him."

"But he's impossible! He brought a party in for billiards the other day and upset Mina's entire schedule. Besides, he brings in such gruesome characters and the place is in a mess afterward. Can't you tell him this is our home too and that he has to let me know when he invites people? Some of them aren't fit for Janna to meet."

"My dear, he is in the secret police. You don't want to get into trouble with the SD."

That always silenced her mother. She seemed to be afraid of Herr Frosch, for she never said anything to his face.

The winter had fled and spring came tiptoeing through the garden, waking a snowdrop here, a crocus there. Soon the place was a riot of color enlivened by a whole orchestra of birdsong. The birds, at least, were happy. Janna asked for a little plot of land, where she sowed radishes and cress. She picked some of the flowers and made wreaths out of them for the mermaids, whom she called her Rhine maidens.

One afternoon the Baron was coming to tea. Otto had an engagement and would not be there, but Mechtild invited Janna to help hand around the cups. It was a lovely day. The March sun was pouring through the windows of the long room, where Janna's mother sat behind the tea table. She was pouring tea from a silver teapot into fragile cups. Her wide sleeves fell away from her slender, shapely arms as she did so. Behind her, on the white marble of the mantelpiece, skillfully carved cupids sported among garlands of grapes. The Baron sat opposite her, talking earnestly.

"You've no idea what we're up against," Janna heard him say. "We do the fighting and bear the losses, but most of the recruits and equipment go to Hitler's favorites, the SS and the air force. None of our formations is complete and we aren't allowed to disband some and bring the remaining up to strength, for that would be bad propaganda. We need not have lost three hundred thousand men at Stalingrad; we wanted to withdraw when we saw it was hopeless, but Hitler ordered us to stay: 'A true Aryan does not turn his back.' It was a massacre...all those fine young men!"

"Can't you *do* something about it?" asked Mechtild. "Talk to someone?" The Baron laughed bitterly.

"To whom? Hitler is not only commander-in-chief of all the armed forces, he is also the supreme ruler of the civilians. He is the 'sole judge of what is good for the German people without being bound by legal regulations.' Besides, all officers of the Wehrmacht had to take a personal oath of unconditional obedience to Hitler. We have marvelous soldiers—it is owing to them that things aren't worse—but if this goes on..."

"Oh dear," said Mechtild.

"Meanwhile, officers are withdrawn from the Russian front to guard against an invasion here," the Baron added. "Including me."

"It's a rest for you...your poor shoulder," said Mechtild soothingly.

"My shoulder can go to blazes. I eat my heart out here, knowing that my fellow officers are getting hell out there."

Mechtild looked up and saw Janna standing in the doorway. "Janna, I didn't see you. Come in," she said. "Have you been listening to Dietrich's wild talk? Don't pay attention to it; he is a great patriot, I assure you."

The Baron got up to greet Janna. "Have you recovered from our night out?" he asked.

"It was very nice," said Janna lamely. She felt uncomfortable with the Baron. What had he said about Hitler?

The Baron sat down and turned to Frau Oster again. "We could have had Russia in our hands," he growled. "In the Caucasus we disbanded the communal farms and established self-government. We had the people all fighting on our side, but Hitler stopped it. No equality for Slavs."

Quite right, thought Janna. The Slavs were inferior. She scowled as she handed the plate of cakes to the Baron, but he did not look at her.

"It's those infernal racial policies that are cooking our goose," he remarked morosely.

There were voices in the anteroom. Frau Oster frowned. The glass doors opened and in stepped Herr Frosch, followed by two natty SS officers. Herr Frosch bowed to Mechtild and introduced his friends: Herr Sturmbannführer Schmidt and Herr Obersturmbannführer Wolff. They had wanted so much to meet the famous Mechtild Oster that he had taken the liberty to bring them. Janna's mother was not a trained actress for nothing. She smiled graciously and asked the gentlemen to sit down. Janna brought extra chairs. The Baron's face froze. He rose and sauntered to the window, his back to the visitors.

"Janna, fetch more cups," Frau Oster said. When Janna returned with a tray holding extra cups and saucers and a second plate of Mina's delicious cakes, she saw that Herr Sturmbannführer Schmidt and Herr Obersturmbannführer Wolff were talking animatedly to her mother while Herr Frosch was quietly consuming the cakes. The Baron still had his back turned to them.

"Forgive me," Herr Obersturmbannführer was saying to Mechtild with boyish enthusiasm, his face flushing into his shining blond hair. "I've seen you as Sieglinde five times and I've seen you every night in *Doll's House* and I've wept, positively *wept*, every time. The beauty of the Aryan wife, her love, her courage…how can you bear such suffering every night?" Mechtild's lips twitched a little as she answered, "A good supper helps. Do have some tea, Herr Sturmbannführer; wouldn't you like a cake, Herr Obersturmbannführer?"

Herr Schmidt was too busy gazing at her. "This is the greatest day of my life…" he said dramatically. "You don't know what a fan I am of yours…I used to pin up your picture in my room. And here I am…face to face…"

Herr Frosch had cleaned up one plate of cakes and was starting on the other. The Baron turned around and silently surveyed the SS officers. There was such contempt in his eyes that Janna felt shocked. They were a bit uncouth, she allowed, but they probably had not had the Baron's advantages. She urged a cake on Herr Wolff before Herr Frosch had eaten them all. The Baron must have repented of his churlishness, for he sat down, handing his cup to Mechtild for more tea. Herr Frosch followed his example.

"Genuine tea," he praised, smacking his lips. Herr Schmidt discovered that his own tea was cooling and hastily drank it, too hastily, for the spoon fell from the saucer to the floor. In diving for it, Herr Schmidt spilled tea on Mechtild's pretty shoe. Straightening up, he apologized profusely and took a cake to cover his confusion. He promptly choked on it. The Baron looked at his wristwatch.

Herr Wolff was blushing at the awkwardness of his companion and rose from his chair. "We'd better not take up more of the *gnädige Frau's* time," he said, clicking his heels. With a sigh Herr Frosch abandoned the last cake. "You're right, we've got work to do," he agreed. They bowed themselves out of the room. Janna ran after them to show them to the front door. She heard the Baron say, "There goes the master race," and her mother answering, "I did not know you were such a snob, Dietrich."

When Janna returned, the Baron was talking again. "…against all rules of decent warfare: shooting and torturing prisoners, murdering old people, babies…no mercy. We've tried to save whom we could, I threatened to shoot it out once with the SS if they did not release the civilians to us, but we are not always there. The cruelties have been unthinkable."

"Perhaps Hitler doesn't know…" began Mechtild timidly. The Baron laughed harshly.

"His orders, Mechtild, don't fool yourself. Inferior races, you see."

"Can't someone stop the SS?"

"We did stop them sometimes, as I said, but we have no jurisdiction over them. They are outside anyone's control—and they have sown a hatred of us in the Russians which our children may have to pay for."

Janna tiptoed off. She did not want to hear more. The Baron's words had upset her badly. She did not want to believe them, but neither could she believe the Baron to be a liar and a traitor, not with all those medals! Was Hitler then not the benevolent ruler she had supposed him to be? And Herr Schmidt and Herr Wolff…were they really cruel? They had such clean, open faces!

Janna wandered about the garden, clenching and twisting her hands, fiddling with her ring. She passed Heinz's secret place and wondered if he was there. She peeped inside but the hideaway was empty. She sat on the chair and looked through the knothole. It was funny how much of the garden you could see with one eye. As usual, it was deserted. She wondered if the neighbors guessed that Heinz was spying on them! There was a rustling noise as Janna saw the little dog come running into the garden. He had a newspaper in his mouth. He was always picking up things. Amused, Janna watched him worrying the paper. The wind flapped it open and Janna could see the letterhead: *Vry Nederland.* That meant *The Free Netherlands.* Startled, she looked again. But...that was one of the forbidden papers, a paper printed by the Dutch Resistance! Herr Frosch often said they should make an example of people caught reading these papers and shoot them. One of the children had followed the dog. It was the girl of her own age. She did not call "Fokkie, Fokkie" out loud as usual. She whispered it, with frightened gestures. The dog came to her, wagging his tail. He'd dropped the paper; she had to go and fetch it. After they had gone into the house, Janna sat for a long time on the chair thinking. Why had she looked? Heinz and his horrible spy hole! She wished she hadn't seen it! Now she did not know whether to tell or not. Herr Frosch did say the people should be shot. Was it really so bad for the Dutch to have their own newspaper? She'd ask her father about it. Meanwhile, she'd keep her mouth shut.

She left the spy hole and went inside. Her father and mother were talking in the hall. The Baron must have left. Her father was holding the evening edition of the German paper, looking grave.

"I'm afraid this will mean reprisals," he said. "We can't let such insubordination pass, we have to keep things under control."

"What's the matter?" asked Janna.

"Nothing, dear," said her mother, putting a hand on her father's arm. "Nothing. Go tell Mina to take away the tea things." Janna trudged discontentedly down the stairs. When were her parents going to treat her like an equal? Probably never, she thought bitterly.

Mina and Corrie were arguing in the kitchen. Janna's Dutch was good enough now so that she could follow their conversation.

"I don't know what you want with a foreign church," Mina was saying.

"It isn't a foreign church..." Corrie answered hotly. "It's as patriotic as any. Didn't they clap our priest in prison for speaking his mind?"

"Yes, they do stand up to the Germans, I'll allow that," Mina conceded graciously.

"And you a Lutheran…" Corrie continued. "Your church was started by a German!"

"There you're wrong," Mina answered with dignity. "I'm now Dutch Reformed." They stopped talking when they saw Janna, who hastily delivered her message under the threat of Mina's eyebrows.

At dinnertime Janna learned what had bothered her parents. Herr Frosch did not seem to think it unfit for her ears.

"I see you read about it," he said, pointing with his fork at the paper by Otto's plate. "Those Dutch renegades burned the registry at Plantage Avenue. They forced their way in, dressed as police, and set it on fire." There was a look of satisfaction on Herr Frosch's face. He'd always *said* the Dutch were bad, and now he was proved right.

"What is a registry?" asked Janna.

"A public registry is where people keep the data of births and deaths. We won't be able to separate the Jews from the Aryans now," her father explained.

Herr Frosch laughed. "That's all taken care of. Holland is free of Jews now except for the last lot in Amsterdam, and they'll be going soon. No, it's labor we need and we have to know who is the right age to call up."

"Did we capture the people who did it? Were they tortured?" asked Heinz with glittering eyes. Janna's parents looked at him with distaste, but his mother bent over him soothingly.

"No, Heinz darling, don't worry. No one was tortured, they all got away." Heinz looked disappointed and stretched out his hand for a cake.

"Eat your vegetables first," said his mother.

"I hate kale." And Heinz spat out a mouthful, which fell like green slime on the white tablecloth.

"Really…" said Frau Oster in an outraged voice, rising from her seat. Herr Oster beckoned her to sit down again.

"Now, Heinz, see what you've done," wailed his mother, making things worse with her napkin. Herr Frosch stared fixedly at his son. A vein in his temple had begun to throb. His eyes were like stones.

"Go to your room and wait for me," he said in an ice-cold voice. Heinz grew pale with fright and ran. Janna, looking at Herr Frosch, suddenly felt scared too.

The Birthday

JANNA LOOKED THROUGH THE WINDOWS of her room at the neighboring children, who were playing in their garden. Several times she had made efforts to befriend them without result. Yet they were at her mercy. If she told they'd been reading an underground Dutch newspaper, terrible things would happen to them. She wondered whether she was a traitor not to tell. She tried to find out from her father.

"What is an underground newspaper?" she asked him.

"Huh, what do you know about that?" Her father looked at her suspiciously.

"Herr Frosch talks about it," Janna said truthfully.

"Herr Frosch talks about everything," her father said irritably. "His mouth is so big, someday he'll swallow himself."

Janna thought that very funny. When she had stopped laughing she said, "Yes, Papa, but tell me now, why is it so bad for the Dutch to have an underground paper?"

"Well," said her father, "it is written by people who oppose our government. They write up everything we do or say in a bad light and they report what they hear over Radio Orange, which is enemy propaganda. You can see how that could interfere with our discipline."

"Will it make us lose the war?" asked Janna. Her father looked at her.

"Whom have you been listening to?" he asked. "We're not going to lose the war. Our armies are too powerful."

"But the Baron says..."

"The Baron!" said her father angrily. "I'm not a bit surprised to hear he is behind this. Those Junkers all feel superior to the ordinary man. They can't stand that they are considered no better than anyone else now. Don't talk to me about the Baron." And her father dove behind his newspaper again. Janna felt her father was unfair to the Baron and had been jumping to conclusions, for she had not told him what the Baron had said. If he was so sure they were going to win, she thought, there was no need to bother him with a little transgression of the neighbors.

Heinz had been hanging around, wanting her to play checkers with him. He was becoming a nuisance. Janna felt sure he was spying on her, as well as on the neighbors. She was forced to lock her door now and walk with the key around her neck. When she forgot, she would find her neat drawers disturbed, dirty footprints on the rug, and sometimes the windows banging when she knew she had shut them. She believed he even invaded her room at night. Once she had woken and felt sure she heard someone else breathing in her room. She stayed quite still; she wasn't going to give Heinz the satisfaction of having scared her.

Now Heinz proved to her that he had been snooping. As she again said she did not want to play checkers, he threatened, "You'd better or I'll have you put in prison." They were standing in the upper hallway opposite one of the "valuable" statues.

"Nonsense," said Janna. "I'm a Hitler Youth. You're not, you can't do anything to me." That was an unkind cut. Heinz wanted nothing so much as to be a Hitler Youth, but he hadn't reached the right age yet.

"It isn't nonsense," Heinz protested. "I've got something of yours that's real bad."

"That's ridiculous," said Janna. "I've never done anything that bad."

"Yes, you have; yes, you have," jeered Heinz, pulling the caricature of

Hitler out of his pocket. Janna realized at once how hard it would be to prove she hadn't done it. She had been sitting at the desk when Heinz had surprised her and he had seen her shoving it into the drawer. The lettering and the words were German. Who would believe it had been drawn by a Dutch girl? She chased after Heinz, trying to grab it, but he was too quick for her. He was waving it in front of her to tease her, and just as she thought she had it, he was off again. He finally locked himself in his room and laughed at her through the transom. The following days she had to play a lot of checkers under threat of the sketch, which annoyed her. She watched for an opportunity to slip into his room and search for it. She found it one morning while he was in his spy hole. She had never been in his room before. It was a large room, larger than hers. It had been furnished by the van Arkels: there was a bookcase full of adventure stories and a lovely model of a sailing ship. But Heinz had superimposed his own treasures. The walls were full of photographs and newspaper clippings of the war and of Youth rallies and marching Jung Volk, and of Hitler making speeches and kissing babies. Above Heinz's bed hung an enormous blood-red flag with a black swastika. On the opposite wall hung a framed text.

"Almighty God," it said. "We don't need Your help, we can take care of ourselves, but please refrain from helping our enemies. Adolf Hitler."

Janna rummaged in Heinz's drawers and closets and searched through the things on the table beside his bed. She could not find the sketch. She kept peering through the window to make sure Heinz was not emerging from his hideaway. She grew more and more desperate, wondering where to look next, as she played nervously with her fingers, sliding her ring up and down. It slipped and fell off, rolling over the floor. Janna crawled after it. It had landed under the bed, and as she groped for it among clumps of dust, her hand touched a piece of paper. She pulled it out along with the ring...yes! It was the missing sketch! She tore it at once into little pieces and put them into her pocket to throw away later. She slipped her ring on again, but she looked at it with awe. Had it wanted to help her? Could there be power in the ring? Was it not just her imagination?

The hunt for the Rembrandt was still going on and Janna was getting bored with it. She did not understand why Hitler wanted it. He ought to be concentrating on winning the war, not looking for pictures. Still, she enjoyed accompanying her mother to the attic, which was a regular storehouse of discarded objects, all suggesting happy days in the van Arkel family.

"Oh, look, Mother, they must have had grand parties...all those Chinese lanterns..." and "Oh Mama, the little cradle...do you think all the children slept in it?" But her mother never answered these questions. Janna was rocking on an old rocking horse one day while her mother searched in trunks and closets.

"Why did the van Arkels leave?" she asked. "If they wanted to move to another house, they would have taken their things with them, wouldn't they?" Her mother rubbed her forehead. "Don't bother me," she said. "I don't know. I think the army requisitioned the house."

"You mean, the family was put out so we could live in their house and use all their things?" Janna asked incredulously.

"I hope not..." said her mother, sounding miserable.

"Did the Baron do it?"

"Oh no, no," her mother said, too quickly. "Not Dietrich. He is much too kind. He'd never do a thing like that..." But Janna wasn't convinced. The Baron was a soldier. He had to kill people. He probably didn't mind taking away their things, that was much less bad than killing them. She had heard of armies plundering. Why should the Baron be different?

"You're not wearing the van Arkel clothes any more," said Mechtild, changing the subject.

"People recognize them," said Janna.

"You're right. It's much better not to wear them. We aren't thieves. I've written down everything we break or use up so we can replace it later."

"Later? You don't think we're going to win the war, do you?" asked Janna, looking sharply at her mother, who flushed and bit her lip.

"You and your father..." she said angrily. "You think only of what men do to you. What does it matter whether we win or lose? Is that going to help us when we die and God asks us what we did with the van Arkel possessions? Have you ever thought of that?" Janna hadn't, and it embarrassed her to have her mother talk in that way. Hildegarde or Kurt would have laughed at her; they thought it superstitious to believe in God...

Mechtild saw Janna's embarrassment and again changed the subject. "You need some clothes of your own," she said. "I can't have you looking like a dust mop. Next week you'll be twelve. I'll take the day off and we'll go shopping."

Janna had not celebrated her birthday since she was nine. Erna had not approved of such a waste of time and money. So on the morning of her twelfth birthday she woke with a feeling of excitement. She wondered whether her mother would remember. She did not expect presents, when they were going to buy clothes, but she hoped for something festive: perhaps pancakes!

When she came down and entered the dining room, she saw that her chair had been decorated with little bunches of violets. At her plate lay a pile of presents. From her mother she got a gold locket and chain. It held a blond curl on one side, from her mother, and a lock of her father's dark hair on the other side. She also got a large signed photograph of the two of them. The Frosches gave her a handkerchief embroidered with swastikas. She had kept the biggest parcel for the last. It was from Heinz. She unwrapped it, layer by layer. At last it ended in a small box. When she opened it, a horrid big spider crawled out, glad to be released from its captivity. Janna gave a yell and dropped the box. The spider scurried over the table, over Mechtild's plate, and over the cheese. Janna's father captured it, opened the window, and released it.

Heinz had been watching all this with satisfaction, until his father boxed his ears. "That'll teach you not to spoil my breakfast," he growled.

"Why didn't you kill it, Otto?" Mechtild asked, shivering.

"A useful insect, the spider," said Otto, unfolding his napkin. "In its place, of course."

"A spider is not an insect," said Herr Frosch pompously. "It has eight legs."

"What would you call it then?" asked Otto. "An octoped?" Herr Frosch mumbled something, he had taken too big a bite of his peanut bun to be intelligible. The Baron had sent a big bag of peanuts, a rare luxury, and they had them three times a day: as a spread, in bread, stirred into curries, or sprinkled over desserts.

Janna was to go shopping with her mother after breakfast. As she put on her old coat, she noticed it was getting too small for her. She could hardly button it. Too much good food. As they were opening the upper hall door, they came face to face with the Baron, who was carrying a bouquet of tulips. Janna and her mother took off their coats again and Corrie was sent for a bottle of sherry and glasses. Janna went to get a vase for the tulips. When she returned, the Baron held out a beautifully wrapped parcel to her, tied with gold ribbon.

"I remembered it was your birthday today," he said, smiling at her.

Janna undid the ribbon and found a dark-red velvet box. Opening it, she saw it was lined with white satin and held a shimmering string of cultured pearls. She stood staring at it, unable to believe it was really hers. Out of the corner of her eye she saw her mother, flushed and trembling, stretch out her hands to the Baron.

"Dietrich, how kind! I do thank you…" The Baron took her hands and held them close to his chest.

"My dear," he muttered.

The velvet box fell out of Janna's hands, the pearls slid along the floor. When Janna had retrieved them and stood up again, her face flushed, the Baron and her mother were talking normally, sipping sherry.

Frau Oster was saying, "I think Herr Frosch suspects me of having done away with the Rembrandt picture."

The Baron frowned. "I wish I hadn't had to land you with those people," he said. "But I could not get out of it. This was the best I could do."

"Yes, yes," Mechtild said hurriedly. "I understand."

When the Baron had left, Janna gave the pearls to her mother. "They're too beautiful," she said. "I don't want to wear them."

Her mother stared at her. Then she said, "Maybe you're right. They are a bit old for you. The locket is better."

"Yes, and that was for *me*," said Janna. "But the Baron gave me the pearls because he wanted to please *you*."

"Don't be a goose," said her mother, blushing.

Janna and her mother finally reached Kalverstraat, that special shoppers' paradise where even before the war no cars were allowed. On the way they passed a round pillar covered with posters and announcements. It caught Janna's eye because there were big pictures on it of her father and mother with an advertisement for their play *My Sister and I*. Under it was an announcement of the Hallensport Festival of the Hitler Youth in the Apollo Hall. Beside it a notice said: "Jews in Holland are not allowed to reside anywhere except in Amsterdam." She remembered the expression on Herr Frosch's face when he said, "The last lot will go soon."

What was happening to these people?

Then she read: "Obligatory application for labor. All men between eighteen and thirty-five years of age who live in occupied Holland's territory and do not have special dispensation must present themselves at their local labor office." Followed by the notice: "The higher SS and police leaders announce that the following have been condemned to death." Several women who were reading the notice wept. There was a long list of names.

Janna's mother was studying something on the other side of the pillar and Janna joined her. It seemed to attract attention; quite a number of people were reading it.

"On the twenty-seventh day of March, 1943," it said, "unknown ruffians wearing the uniforms of Amsterdam police, after attacking the guards, broke into the public registry at Plantage Avenue, Amsterdam, and set fire to the place with incendiary material. Any information that can lead to the discovery of the criminals should be given to the German and Dutch police. To discover the perpetrators, the higher SS and police commands have offered a ten-thousand-gulden award. SS Sturmbannführer Lages."

"Those boys must be far away, if the Germans are offering so much money," came the quivering voice of an elderly gentleman who was gazing at the announcement.

"What do you mean, so much money?" snapped a skinny old lady who was wearing one black and one brown shoe, tied with string. She blew her nose in a piece of newspaper. "I would not betray someone for less than a pound of prewar coffee."

"Or a loaf of prewar bread," agreed another woman. "They take our good food and give us their dirty money."

Frau Oster hurriedly pulled Janna away. They crossed the Mint square, where barges carrying a colorful array of spring flowers lay moored in the canal. Entering Kalverstraat, they sauntered past shops which were anything but tempting. Everywhere were signs of dilapidation: peeling paint, torn window shades, windowpanes cracked and mended with tape. Frau Mueller had been right: the merchandise looked shoddy, skimpily cut, of artificial material. Yet shabbily dressed people stood in line to buy it, clutching their coupons. Janna noticed that there were very few young men about, apart from those in uniform.

"I suppose they've all gone to work in Germany," said her mother. They left Kalverstraat and crossed the Dam, which Frau Oster said got its name from the dam erected to protect the first settlers from the sea. Now it was a big square in front of the palace paved with large cobbles called "children's heads" in Holland.

Janna did not much care for the gray, square, unromantic palace, which bore no resemblance to the turreted castles of Germany. Her mother said it was a good Renaissance building, designed as a town hall. It became a palace much later. It was filled with French furniture left there by Louis Napoleon, who had once occupied the same position Seyss-Inquart held now.

A group of children stood looking at a Punch and Judy show. There were bursts of laughter, and more and more grownups came to join the children.

"I believe this is a regular institution," said Janna's mother. "It's a tradition to have this show here. Let's look at it."

Punch, who was called Jan Klaassen in Holland, was trying on a lot of hats, but none seemed to fit. They were all too large.

"I'm trying to get a V," he said, holding up his hand with his fingers in the V position, "but all I'm getting is six and a quarter [*zes en'n kwart*]."

There were howls of laughter and it wasn't hard to figure that *zes en'n kwart* sounded like Seyss-Inquart.

"I don't think we should listen to this, dear," said Janna's mother, trying to pull her away. "It's political."

"It's funny, Mother," said Janna. "Just another minute..."

Jan Klaassen was now standing absolutely still, with his arm up in the Hitler salute. The audience waited, not knowing what to make of it.

"That's how high my doggie jumps when he greets me in the evening..." said Jan Klaassen, which raised a storm of delight. Katryn, Jan Klaassen's wife, now joined him. She was reading a newspaper.

"Dear, dear," she muttered. "Those English and Americans, they're so stupid. They never hit munition plants, or railways, or harbors. All they ever do with their bombs is kill cows. I hear Hitler is going to put up a statue to the Unknown Cow." More laughter. Coins began to tinkle on the pavement. Now a gaunt character appeared, clad in a white nightshirt with a sleeping cap on his head. He represented Death and was affectionately called Pierlala. In the traditional show he was always after the landlord and ended up stuffing him into a coffin, but this time Pierlala had no coffin.

"There's a shortage," he explained. "The Germans took them all. They need them at the Russian front." There was thunderous applause. A policeman approached to inspect the noise.

Jan Klaassen hastily asked, "For whom?"

"For the Russians, of course," said Pierlala unctuously. "You know the Germans have come to save us from the Russians, don't you? They are *taking* measures to save us from what the Russians would take. They are thieves, those Russians!" When the policeman had strolled out of earshot, Pierlala said quickly, "Every night Hitler thanks God for the Russians. If they did not exist, he'd have to invent them."

The laughter was uproarious and Janna's mother shivered.

"Come on," she said to Janna, "this is disgraceful. You should not listen to it. They are making fun of us." Janna left reluctantly. She dearly wanted to know what Jan Klaassen would say next.

"Don't say anything about this at home," warned her mother. "We don't want more trouble than there is already."

"No, I won't tell," said Janna. Then, with a rush, "Mother, I noticed something about the neighbors..."

"Don't tell me," her mother said quickly. "I don't want to know."

They went to a large department store called the Beehive and there, after a lot of waiting in line, Frau Oster bought Janna a navy-blue coat and hat, and a red dress. Frau Oster had to pay a lot of coupons, which came out of her own clothes allowance, so Janna was grateful.

"May I keep them on?" she begged, admiring herself in the mirror.

"You'd better," said her mother. "I don't want to see you in those rags any more." She gave Janna's old clothes to the saleslady, who was very happy to get them.

"They will fit Anneke, my little girl," she said, tears in her eyes. "I was just wondering how I was going to dress her, she has grown out of *everything*. You don't know what you have done for me." It made Janna a little ashamed.

When they left the Beehive, her mother said wistfully, "I'd like to take you to a restaurant for coffee as my mother used to do on my birthdays, but unless we paid the black-market price, all we'd get is colored water. What we could do, since we have no parcels to carry, is to take a walk through the old city and visit the house where Rembrandt lived. I'd like you to see it; it's typical of his period and full of his etchings."

"I'd like that," said Janna.

It was a lovely spring day. The old city, with its narrow streets and humped bridges, looked its best. Elm and linden trees leaned over the canals with their lazily undulating water, and the dark brick houses, topped by scalloped gables, leaned too. Frau Oster explained that this was done on purpose.

"Their doors and passages are so narrow that the burghers have to hoist their furniture through the windows. Do you see the lengths of beam sticking out at the top of the gables, with hooks on them? People haul up their furniture by slinging a rope around the hook, and because the house leans forward, the furniture swings clear."

A loud singing interrupted their conversation. Boots came ringing and clacking over the cobbles. A company of uniformed men passed, slouching, not quite in step. They were not Wehrmacht soldiers nor were they police. They wore three-cornered insignia on their sleeves with the letters N.S.B. The man in front carried a banner with horizontal stripes of orange, white, and baby blue.

"Who are they?" asked Janna.

"Those are members of the Dutch National Socialist Bund," said Frau Oster. "A person called Anton Mussert is their leader." So those were the Mussert boys Corrie had been complaining about.

"Who is Mussert?"

"He was made head of the Netherlands by Hitler last December."

"I thought Seyss-Inquart was head here," said Janna.

"Of course. Mussert only got a courtesy title, to reward him for helping us. He has no power at all, except over his own men. The Dutch hate him and his crowd more than they hate us. There is no doubt that they help us to control the Dutch civilians with a minimum of our own forces."

"You don't like them?"

"Does anyone like traitors? Besides, they are no good. Many volunteered to go to Russia, but we had to send them back again. Look at the way they march!"

Even after the Mussert men were out of sight, the street still seemed to ring with the sound of their boots.

A pale April sun smiled faintly down, reflected in the canals. Light-green sprouting leaves shone tenderly against the deep magenta of the old houses, with their shutters and stoops and small-paned windows. A few seagulls wheeled screeching over the water and up into the sky again. A long barge was churning mud out of a canal with metal cups which whirred around on a belt, scooping the mud into the barge and going back empty into the water again. Janna and her mother watched for a while, but the stench chased them away.

A few hopeful youngsters were fishing from a bridge, their eyes intent on their lines, little pails standing ready for their catch. A woman shook out a mat from an open window, making the dust fly. She called a greeting to the bargeman, who shouted back. An errand boy rattled past on a dilapidated bicycle which looked as if it were held together by strings. As they sauntered on, Janna and Frau Oster came to an archway where a charitable organization was distributing soup. A long line of people stood waiting patiently, holding empty bowls in their hands. Janna saw pale, thin faces, etched with suffering, hollow eyes, skinny legs. She smelled cabbage, and peering into a pot she saw thin, watery soup. Some people in the line complained it wasn't worth waiting for, it didn't fill you for long.

"Even a little is better than nothing," mumbled a toothless old man.

As they went on, Janna was thinking. "Why is there such a shortage of food here?" she asked. "Have they no farms?"

"They are helping to feed our army now," her mother said in a low voice. "We requisition their food."

"But...isn't that stealing?" asked Janna.

"We've had shortages for a long time ourselves, it's natural to think of our own people first," said her mother.

Janna stared at her. "If I were Dutch, I'd hate us!" she said. Her mother was silent.

They had come to a street which was roped off. An SS soldier, heavily armed, refused to let them pass.

"We only want to see the house where Rembrandt lived," pleaded Frau Oster.

"Impossible. Against orders," said the guard.

"But I was here only last month..."

"It is forbidden," said the guard. Frau Oster looked worried as she and Janna retraced their steps.

"Those are the Jewish quarters," she said in a trembling voice. "What are they doing to those unfortunate people?" Her footsteps dragged. Suddenly a scream pierced the air. It came from the dark alleys behind them—a scream of such wild despair, such pain, that Janna and Frau Oster stood as if glued to the ground. It was followed by another and again another, corkscrewing into the skies. Janna twisted her hands together...she could not bear it...There were some shots, then silence.

Janna's mother seemed to be sagging. She was deathly pale.

"I've got my headache again," she moaned. "And I forgot to bring aspirin."

"Let's go to the nearest tram stop," Janna suggested. Her legs were trembling and she was feeling sick herself. "Lean on me." She supported her mother and they walked slowly across a bridge. When they were away from the Jewish quarters, Mechtild began to feel better.

As they waited for a tram, Janna marveled at the strange transportation in Amsterdam. There were bicycle taxis for one passenger, old motorcars pulled by cadaverous horses, carts of all shapes and sizes. A fine, aristocratic lady, dressed in silk and holding a parasol, sat in a velvet armchair on top of a handcart. She was being pushed by a chauffeur in gold-braided livery.

"That's what I call keeping up appearances," said Janna's mother, smiling. The sight seemed to revive her.

The first tram that passed was a special. It was decorated with garlands of tulips and daffodils. Inside sat a bride and bridegroom in all their finery. The other seats were filled with waiting guests. Someone was playing an accordion. It seemed a merry party.

"How clever," said Frau Oster, looking herself again. "I suppose they can't rent a car so they're doing it this way. I've noticed," she added, "that the Dutch are not the staid people I always believed them to be. They seem to take a childish pleasure in festivities, rather like the Italians."

Another tram arrived. Janna and her mother got in. Everyone seemed to be looking at a portly businessman smoking a cigar. He seemed to enjoy this, and leaned back, dramatically puffing out rings of smoke, which drifted like the ghosts of pretzels through the carriage. The man sitting opposite breathed in the scent with an ecstatic face and closed eyes. He leaned over to the smoker.

"That looks like a nice cigar," he said. "I wouldn't mind paying fifty gulden for one of them. Have you any to spare?"

"Do you mean it?" asked the smoker.

"I do."

"Then I can give you ten."

"Done." The owner of the cigar handed over a box of ten and the other gentleman gave him a wad of banknotes. The people in the tram looked on with various expressions of envy, disapproval, and amusement.

The tram stopped and Janna and her mother got out. They had not dared to say a word in the tram for fear of betraying their nationality. Now they walked home silently, each wrapped in her own thoughts. As they rounded a corner and entered the Keizer's canal, the street where they lived, they saw a woman wheeling a pram. Her clothes were threadbare but clean; her face, with its skin tightly drawn over delicate bones, had a certain beauty. There was a proud, defiant lilt to her walk, something queenly. The baby in the rickety pram resembled a shriveled monkey with liquid brown eyes. He was dwarfed by an enormous yellow star. The woman wore one too.

"Those are Jews..." Janna said it wonderingly. They weren't in the least like the pictures she had seen of Jews.

"Yes," said Frau Oster nervously. "They should not be here, they're not allowed out of their ghetto..."

Janna's thoughts were in a muddle. She remembered the teaching at school: "Jews are dangerous; they deserve all they're getting..." How could a little baby not a month old deserve anything... or be dangerous?

There was an echoing noise as two SS officers on motorcycles stank up the air. They looked like black beetles under the fresh green of the trees. When they saw the young woman, they uttered coarse German curses. A fanatical fury distorted their faces. They shouted at her to stop. Leaving their motorcycles, they grabbed her by the arm and shook her. They pointed to the inner city and told her to go where she belonged. They said the next time they'd shoot, and kill the baby first. One of the officers struck the woman in the face. The other pulled her hair. She never said a word, but quietly went where they told her. The men kicked her and made her run. The poor baby bounced up and down and began to wail, a thin sliver of sound slicing the air. The woman was holding a handkerchief to her face. It was red with blood.

Janna clung to her mother in terror. Frau Oster was trembling. The SS officers caught sight of her. They straightened their caps and their faces and for the first time Janna recognized them. They were Obersturmbannführer Wolff and Sturmbannführer Schmidt.

"Mechtild!" they cried, cordially approaching Janna's mother. "We saw you in *My Sister and I* last night. You were superb…" They kissed Frau Oster's fingertips. They had been transformed in a twinkling from brutes into gallants.

Janna felt a sense of shock, a numbing of sensation. As her mother conversed glibly with the officers, charming and gracious, Janna felt as if something had cracked under her feet…as if the firm ground no longer supported her. And her mother…her mother was a stranger.

Lessons

Janna waited impatiently for Hugo. There were things she had to ask him. No one else would give her a real answer. She knew there was injustice somewhere. The Dutch were not being treated fairly, and as for the Jews... She gave a little shudder.

Little things she had observed, little drops and trickles, were flowing together and making a stream on which she was floating she knew not where.

What was the matter with grownups, who had all the power? Why did they not do something? Why did they draw blinds and chatter with monsters? Rebelliously she thought that all children ought to get together and disown the grownups. But would that help? Had the Children's Crusade accomplished anything?

Perhaps Corrie was right. You had to start on yourself, with your own conscience. But what if you didn't *know* enough? Which brought her back to Hugo. So she waited for him, peering out of the library window, shooing off Heinz, who wanted to play checkers again.

As Hugo entered the library, it struck her how frail he looked, almost as if his body were incapable of carrying the weight of his thoughts. He sank into his leather chair with a sigh of relief, took off his glasses and rubbed them, his mild brown eyes contemplating the room.

"Yesterday," Janna began with a rush, "yesterday I was out with my mother and I...we...saw starving people and we couldn't get into the

Rembrandt house because the guard wouldn't let us. I heard awful screams and later I...we...saw a woman and a little baby wearing stars and the SS officers hit her and kicked her and were *awful* to her and she hadn't done anything except walk. They said they would *shoot* her, even the baby!" Hugo looked at her questioningly. He did not seem surprised or shocked. "Well?" he asked quietly.

"Well, it isn't what I learned...At school they said Hitler was helping the poor democracies who had become so weak they could not stand up to Russia. They said Jews were dangerous people who were being sent to some other place where they could do no harm. But how can babies be dangerous? And that woman, she didn't look dangerous either. They said all Aryans wanted to belong to Germany, and it isn't true, they don't. I don't blame them, for it seems to me...it seems to me..." She hung her head, played with her fingers. "We've only come...to rob them..." she whispered.

Hugo sat very still. Janna looked up with tears in her eyes. "You've explained so much to me, can't you explain this?"

Hugo gave a deep sigh. "I promised your parents I would not discuss politics," he said.

"I would not tell on you," Janna answered indignantly. He was her last hope. She trusted his honesty more than that of anyone else she knew.

"I know that," said Hugo gently. "It is not fear that is keeping me back. It just so happens that I value my word."

"How will I ever learn the truth then?" asked Janna despondently.

"The way other people learn it," said Hugo. "Do you think newspaper reporters find it easy to learn the truth? They may have to interrogate many liars, sift the facts, and draw their own conclusions. Or judges... think of their difficulties; yet a human life may depend on what they decide. Then take scientists, how many years of patient observation it takes them to find out the tiniest truth about our universe. You want to be spoon-fed. You've just learned that you may not have the true idea of what is going on and you want to spend no thought and effort on it yourself. That's a bad attitude. There's a library full of information right here...with enough books in German for you to do some research. Besides, your Dutch is getting good. You have brains, use them." He took off his glasses and polished them again.

Janna looked at him indignantly. "You talk as if there was *time*," she said. "But there's injustice going on *right now* and I don't want to be unjust. I want to *know*." She looked fiercely at Hugo. He smiled.

"What do you want to know?" he asked.

"Are Aryans the master race?"

"I believe I can answer that," said Hugo. "It's an anthropological question. There's no such thing as an Aryan race, except in legends. There's an Aryan language spoken by Hindus and other Indo-Iranian people. It's also loosely used to designate Indo-European people, but it's unscientific to call it a *race*. There are few pure races and it would be bad if there were. I don't know whether you've heard of inbreeding?"

"Yes, the farmers used to talk about it," said Janna.

"It happens to old families, especially royal ones who won't marry commoners. The bad genes multiply and are not counteracted by good ones. The more varied our ancestry, the more vigorous we tend to be."

"Were the Jews inbred, is that why they're inferior?" asked Janna.

"The Jews are not inferior," said Hugo. "A greater percentage of Jews reach prominence than of any other people. They were civilized when we still walked in bearskins and gnawed bones. We have only just begun to enact the humane laws the Jews have obeyed for centuries."

"But...but they killed Jesus, didn't they?" asked Janna.

"Have you never read the Bible?" Hugo asked gently. "The Romans killed Jesus. The Jews never crucified anybody; such a cruel death was not on their books. They condemned Jesus, after a trial, because they did not understand his closeness to God. They thought it blasphemous when he said, 'I and my Father are one.' But they lived in an occupied country like

Holland. They had to deliver Jesus to the Roman authorities, who could have released Jesus had they so wished. We do not blame the present-day Italians for his death, do we? Don't forget, all the first Christians were Jews. We Gentiles have been grafted on the root of Judaism, and in his letters to the Romans, St. Paul tells us not to boast of that, for the root bears the branches, not the other way around. These are mysteries, not to be talked of lightly. The Jews have a very special relationship with God. As St. Paul says again, 'God hath not cast away His people which He foreknew.' They bear testimony to God's holiness, where we are inclined to be a little too familiar. I think they have a mission just as much as the Christians—and how you Germans dare point a finger at them when you condemn millions to death without a trial…" Hugo bit his lip. "I beg your pardon. I had no right to say that."

"I don't mind," said Janna. "I want the truth."

"And you think you can get the truth from me?" asked Hugo. "You might as well ask a chicken the truth about the fox."

"It might be truer than the fox's own story," said Janna.

Hugo laughed. "You may be right at that," he admitted.

"But why do people dislike the Jews then?" asked Janna.

Hugo reflected for a moment. "It's part of the mystery," he said. "They have always been kept apart, a chosen people, and perhaps that dislike was necessary to keep them from melting with the crowd. But there is another reason. They are a minority in all countries, and minorities are often resented and persecuted. As soon as we ill-use people, our conscience troubles us and we have to justify our mistreatment by believing they deserve it. I'm sure you've heard the Germans say that the Dutch are bad."

"Yes," said Janna, struck. "I have. How do you know?"

"For the same reason," said Hugo. Janna felt confused. So much of what she had been taught was being overturned.

"What else do you want to know?" asked Hugo.

"About the last war," said Janna in a rush. "Did we really win it and did the Jews in Berlin stab us in the back by signing the Treaty of Versailles?"

"That's a political question," said Hugo.

"No, it's in our history and race-science books," protested Janna.

Hugo smiled. "You're a minx," he said. "The Allies and Germany had got into a stalemate on the battlefields after three years of ghastly bloodshed in the trenches. When fresh, enthusiastic, well-equipped American soldiers arrived, the exhausted Germans were soon beaten. There was a peace conference among the Allied heads of state to which Germany was not invited. It accepted the resulting treaty under protest, as there was nothing else for it to do." Hugo got up and fetched an encyclopedia, which he opened at the words: *Versailles, treaty of...* "You could have found that out for yourself. It's all in here, see?"

Janna kicked the leg of the table in a burst of temper. "Why did they lie to us at school?" she asked. "It isn't fair!"

"Careful!" warned Hugo. "Don't make sweeping accusations. The teachers may very well have believed what they told you. It is much easier to believe lies than the truth."

"Why?" asked Janna.

"Because lies are manufactured to satisfy the emotions. A mother would rather believe her pretty girl lazy than accept the fact that she's a dumb cluck. Germans would rather believe they were stabbed in the back than that they lost a fair fight. And anyone would rather blame someone else for his misfortunes. The truth is hard. Don't fool with it unless you realize that."

Here there was an interruption. Corrie came in, smiling broadly and bearing a tray with coffee and sandwiches for Hugo. He was a great favorite in the kitchen. Janna noticed the eagerness with which Hugo tackled the food. Was he starving too?

After the lesson, when Hugo was gone, Janna darted to the bookshelves to search for a German Bible. She found a Dutch one, but the words were too hard for her. She knew her mother had a little German Bible beside her bed, but Janna was shy about asking for it. She finally found an old German Bible bound in scuffed leather on the rare-book shelf. She peeped at it with trepidation, feeling wicked. It was a forbidden book for Hitler Youth.

The language awed and gripped her, so that she began to read in earnest. Right away she stumbled on a difficulty: God's treatment of Cain. Cain slew Abel brutally, for no reason. Janna wanted God to slay Cain in return. Instead, He held a long conversation with Cain and merely banished him, which was the least He could do, thought Janna, since Adam and Eve probably did not want him around any more. Cain even had the effrontery to point out to God that others might kill him, presumably his brothers, for who else was there? And God put a sign on Cain to warn people not to kill him. Why did He do that, with Abel's blood crying to heaven?

Janna did not talk to her parents about her conversation with Hugo. Ever since the outing on her birthday, there had been a barrier. She avoided her parents. They were always busy anyway. The Baron came often and took them to cocktail parties to meet important people. Janna was left to brood by herself.

Herr Frosch brought friends in more and more often. Janna's mother complained about it. She said there was no one to keep an eye on Janna at night. She told Janna to stay away from the parties. But Janna was lonely. One evening she felt especially depressed. She had a headache and wandered desolately through the house. It was Mina's night off; she always went to visit a relative. There was no one Janna could talk to, no one to cheer her up. There were sounds of laughter and merriment coming from the long room and she drifted toward it. At that moment she felt that even Herr Frosch was better than nothing. She peeped around the glass doors. What she saw reminded her of those Dutch pictures where everyone is laughing and drinking and spilling food. The beautiful room was in a mess. Herr Frosch was plying his friends with drink. Gaily dressed ladies, showing fat legs, were being kissed and teased. One of the SS officers was boasting of his day's work.

"You should have seen the last batch we got out of that Jewish men's home...with their silly beards and skullcaps! 'Hop like frogs,' I said, and, *zum Teufel*, they did...If they didn't, I helped them with the butt of my gun. 'Bark like dogs'...sure enough, they did...They have no pride, those Jews." He spat on the parquet floor. The others all laughed noisily and emptied their glasses. One of the SS men noticed Janna standing in the doorway and beckoned to her.

"Come in, come in," he shouted. "We can use a pretty girl..." He was grinding out the stub of his cigarette with his heel. Janna never could understand afterward why she obeyed him...had he hypnotized her? She felt as if she were dreaming, as if an outside force were pulling her into the room. The officers all welcomed her, calling her darling and sweetheart. Someone handed her a glass with a drink in it that made her throat sting, but it did revive her a little. Then one of the SS men grabbed her and pulled her onto his lap. He tried to make her kiss him. The dream had turned into a nightmare. Janna struggled feverishly, but the SS man held on. The others all laughed and encouraged him. One of the woman shrilled, "You'll get used to it, deary!"

Janna panicked. "For God's sake, let me go..." she shouted.

"God?" the soldier sneered. "God doesn't exist, or we would not be here."

Holding her tight, he pressed wet lips against her mouth. His breath smelled awful. Then Janna bit his lip hard. He cursed and pushed her off his knees.

"Vixen," he growled, and kicked her. His lip bled. The others only laughed. Herr Frosch, who had been mixing drinks, came hurrying toward them.

"Herr Oberführer," he cried. "That's the daughter of the house, a friend of the general!" There was an immediate hush, but Janna had fled already. She was sick in the bathroom and spent a lot of time rinsing out her mouth.

The next day Janna had a fever. Her mother fetched a doctor who prescribed lots of liquid and bed rest. For the first time, Janna realized how much her parents loved her. Mechtild let an understudy take over while she stayed at Janna's bedside. Otto came in with amusing stories about the theater. Mina cooked her favorite dishes. Even Heinz brought her daffodils he had picked in the garden. Her mother took them but sent Heinz away.

"The doctor says she must be kept quiet," she explained.

Janna had never been so cherished. Her mother read to her from famous plays, which her beautiful voice brought to life. They held discussions afterward. Janna confessed that she'd like to become an actress, and after that her mother let her read parts in plays and corrected her expression. Janna began to feel guilty about her former critical attitude and her secrets weighed on her.

"Mother," she said, when they were having an especially intimate talk, "it isn't right, is it, to maltreat the Jews? Whether we like them or not, it isn't right?"

"No," whispered her mother. "It isn't right."

"But you didn't say so…you were kind to those SS officers…"

"I wondered when you'd come out with that," said her mother. "I knew what you were thinking then, but what could I have done for that poor woman? I could only have made trouble for us. Anyone who takes the part of the Jews is treated like a Jew. I'm a coward, I admit it." Janna began to cry. "I'm bad too, I was disobedient," she said. And she told her mother what had happened at Herr Frosch's party. Her mother was very upset.

"I can't stop Herr Frosch from bringing those people in," she said. "It's his house too. But don't…don't ever join them again, and lock your door at night."

Janna nodded. She never wanted to come within arm's length of an SS man again. Then she told her mother, "That officer said there was no God because, if there was, he himself would not exist." She expected her mother to react indignantly to this impious remark; instead she looked thoughtful.

"Did he really say that?" she mused. Janna nodded. "Poor boy," said her mother.

"Why do you call him poor?" asked Janna resentfully.

"Because he would not say that if he did not think himself very bad," her mother answered. "He thinks God, if He existed, would already have struck him dead."

"God did not strike Cain dead," said Janna. "Why didn't He? Cain murdered his brother, but God only banished him."

"Do you think death would have been the greater punishment?" her mother asked.

"Yes," said Janna.

"That's because you are young. When you are older, you'll learn that death can be a friend. It would have been the easy way out for Cain, though he did not realize that when he pleaded with God to spare him. Perhaps he had to learn what life was like without Abel." Janna flung her arms around her mother's neck.

"I love you," she whispered. Her mother kissed her back.

"I'm glad we're friends again," she said. Janna looked at her, surprised.

"Did you know?" she asked.

"Did you think a mother wouldn't know?"

Janna was getting better. The doctor said she could get up the next day. Corrie usually brought up Janna's tray of food. On the last evening Corrie brought up her dinner, and after she had eaten it, her mother came up with another tray.

"A second dinner?" asked Janna. "I've already had mine."

Her mother looked surprised. "But this tray was standing in the kitchen, ready to be brought up. I saw it when I went to tell Mina something. She wasn't there and I thought I'd save Corrie the trouble."

"Maybe Heinz is ill too," suggested Janna.

"Heinz is in excellent health," said her mother. "He managed to get most of the pudding."

"Perhaps Mina forgot that Corrie had already brought me a tray."

"That's possible. Corrie may have made you one on her own, without Mina knowing about it. Could you tackle another one?"

"I'll try," said Janna. Her mother smiled. Janna's appetite had come back!

When her mother had left, Janna accidentally shifted her plate a little and discovered a paper package. It contained a razor blade. A *razor blade!* Now what in the world would that be doing on Janna's tray? Razor blades were precious. Herr Frosch was constantly complaining of their scarcity and threatening to grow a beard. Janna's father was better off with his old-fashioned knife.

Was it another prank of Heinz's? But what a senseless one! Janna put the blade on the table beside her bed and promptly forgot about it. When she remembered it the next morning, the razor blade was gone.

Sef

THE FIRST MORNING JANNA WAS UP, there was a surprise waiting for her at the breakfast table. Heinz told her about it even before she saw it lying by her plate.

"There's a letter for you," he said enviously. "May I have the stamp?"

Janna did not want to read it with everyone looking on, so she put it in her pocket. It was probably an answer from Hildegarde.

Then she listened, alarmed, to what Herr Frosch was reading from the morning paper. The owner of the Punch and Judy show on the Dam had been arrested.

"No..." she cried, "oh no..."

Herr Frosch frowned at her. "It's a good thing," he said. "I hear his talk was very subversive. There is too much rebellion in this city. Herr Rauter thinks it's the fault of the Dutch Army we allowed to demobilize. It's working underground now."

"How can it work underground?" Frau Frosch asked dreamily. "The ground is too soft. They build their houses on wooden piles, which they hammer into the mud. I've seen them."

Her husband looked at her coldly. "Women should not talk," he said. "They only show their ignorance. Underground is just a manner of speaking. It means hidden. Please make me another piece of toast, Jodoca, you let this one burn. Those people think they are heroic but they are merely foolish. Hand me the sausages, *gnädige Frau,* please. They are done just as they should be, crisp and not greasy. How fortunate we are in having such a good cook. Herr Rauter is always complaining of his servants." Herr Frosch wiped his mouth. "As I was saying, what can a handful of Dutchmen do against our Wehrmacht? The whole idea of resistance is a product of weak democracies. Look what Gandhi is getting from the British by fasting! Ridiculous. We'd just let him die. You must be ruthless. Stop kicking the table, Heinz, you annoy me."

After breakfast Janna went upstairs to read her letter. When she entered her room, she felt a draft and saw that her glass doors were open. She thought she had shut them. She put her letter on the bed and stepped out on the balcony. She heard a rustling in the ivy. Could a prowler climb up that way? Looking closely, she saw spikes sticking out of the wall, between the ivy, forming a ladder. In a twinkling she was over the balcony railing, climbing down. It was scary. Her feet had to feel for the spikes while she hung on to the ivy strands, which sometimes broke loose. When she landed in the garden, she saw no one. Only the neighbors' tomcat blinked at her from a clump of daffodils. Not wanting to climb up again, Janna went into the house and up the stairs. She found the door of her room open and Heinz sprawled on the bed, reading her letter. He had opened it so clumsily that the envelope was badly torn. Its stamp was missing. He did not look in the least ashamed on seeing her but greeted her with a jeer: "Janna's got a boy friend, Janna's got a boy friend!" Janna flew into a rage. She attacked Heinz, dragged him off the bed, shook him, regardless of his kicking feet, pulled his hair, scratched his face, and yelled "Horrible sneak!" She pushed him out of the room, locked the door, and leaned against it, suddenly weak and spent. She could hear Heinz trudging upstairs, wailing for his mother.

Almost crying, Janna picked up the crumpled letter and smoothed it out. Now she understood what Heinz had meant. It wasn't from Hildegarde at all, it was from Kurt.

Dear Janna,

Hildegarde tells me that you are homesick for the Black Forest. I can well imagine it. A flat country must be very dull. Do you go for hikes there at all? We miss you. The rehearsals for the play went badly. Ilse is making such a hash of Brunhilde, I have trouble not laughing, which doesn't help my acting. Anyway I may not get to play Siegfried after all. I've volunteered to go to Russia, they've lowered the age limit.

Don't worry about the Dutch. They'll come around when we've beaten the English and Americans and they have no one else to look to. They'll soon realize the aims and ideals of our Third Reich. They are good, Nordic people.

Please don't forget me, and write...

Affectionately,
Your friend Kurt

P.S. I'll be going to a training camp soon.

Janna sat with the letter in her lap. She found it hard to sort out her emotions. For a moment she had been transported to the old, safe world of the Black Forest. But it seemed very far away now. How happy she would have been with this letter even a few weeks ago! Now it was too late. Poor Kurt, going into the hell of Russia... she remembered what the Baron had said about it. Giving his life for... for a parcel of lies? Germany hadn't a chance of winning there, according to the Baron.

She was not allowed to brood for long. Heinz was banging on the door.

"Let me in, I've got to tell you something!"

"I don't want to hear it," said Janna.

"You must, Mother says so."

With a sigh, Janna got up and unlocked the door. She felt ashamed when she saw his swollen, scratched face.

"Mother says I did wrong. I'm sorry," he mumbled quickly. Then he went on, "But you're horrid too, you won't play with me!"

"I've been ill," said Janna.

"I could have played checkers with you; why didn't you *ask* for me? Your mother would have let me in if you'd *asked* for me." He sounded aggrieved. He looked babyish with his swollen face. Janna pitied him.

"I'll play with you now," she said, feeling she had something to make up for.

"Do you mean it? I've nothing to do. Mother has no time for my lessons." Hugo wasn't coming either. Janna's mother felt she wasn't well enough for studying yet. Janna missed him. It seemed ages since her last lesson.

"But you must behave yourself," said Janna. "I don't want to be ordered about."

"All right, we'll be equals," Heinz said magnanimously. Since he was willing to forgo his masculine superiority, Janna quietly pocketed her extra years.

"Do you want to play in the garden?" she asked.

"No, it's going to rain. Let's play hide-and-go-seek in the house… one hides and the other one seeks. When the hider is found, we race to the nearest banister and whoever gets there first wins."

It proved an amusing game. It was a lovely house to hide in. Janna was touched by Heinz's pleasure. He seemed starved for a little fun. She thought it must be a lonely life for a little boy who hated books. She let him win several times. The third time Heinz hid in the kneehole of the library desk. When Janna spotted him, he ran to the banister, but in his haste he bumped against one of the valuable statues. It fell with a crash onto the tiles. Its head broke off and rolled a little farther. Janna and Heinz contemplated the disaster in silent dismay. Janna thought of her mother's distress that one of the sacred van Arkel possessions should have been broken. Heinz's cheeks had paled till they were almost the color of the statue. They both awaited the inevitable arrival of the angry grownups, summoned by the noise, and braced themselves against reproaches, but no one came.

Heinz raised the statue and replaced the head. It fit nicely, you could hardly see the crack.

"I can glue it," he said hopefully. "My mother has strong glue. No one must know. You won't tell?" He looked anxiously at Janna.

"Not if you don't want me to," said Janna. "I'm not a tattletale. But why are you afraid? Your parents wouldn't punish you for an accident, would they?"

"My father would," said Heinz. "Look." He pulled up his sweater and showed his back full of scars from vicious beatings. Janna recoiled.

"Does he do that often?" she asked, remembering the screams she had thought were the tantrums of a spoiled boy.

"Pretty often," said Heinz.

"Why does your mother let him?"

"She is more scared of him than I am," said Heinz. "I think he beats her too. I *hate* my father." He looked and sounded so ugly, it scared Janna.

"Why don't you behave better, if your father is so strict?" she asked.

"He can't cow *me*," Heinz growled. "The more he beats me, the worse I'll be. I'll show him!" Janna wondered at him. She would have been careful not to annoy so cruel a father. It was brave of Heinz. Maybe there was something fine in Heinz after all.

"Let's go on with the game," said Heinz. Janna proposed continuing it on the third floor, where there were no statues to break. It was her turn and the best hiding place she could think of was her own wardrobe. She hid behind Nella's dresses and leaned against the back panel. She wasn't comfortable and pushed and shoved a little. A small hard knob pressed into her shoulder blades. She groped for it with her fingers, twisting it accidentally. There was a *click*, the back panel swung away—and Janna felt herself falling into space.

For a moment she lay stunned. She had fallen smack onto a hard surface. She opened her eyes in a greenish twilight and found a face bent over her—a pale, angry face—while a voice whispered in Dutch, "What are you doing here? How did you get here?"

She felt too dizzy and scared to answer. Her throat felt dry. Strong hands pulled her upright and shoved her against the wall, pinning her arms. The boy's face looked desperate. His straight red-blond hair was badly cut, his skin looked waxen.

"How did you find this room?" he asked, shaking her till her head banged against the wall.

"I...I was playing hide-and-seek," said Janna hoarsely, in her best Dutch, looking at the boy with terrified eyes.

"I could kill you," the boy went on, "except that people would go looking for you and find me anyway. But I warn you, if you ever breathe a word to anyone that you've seen me, I'll kill you...Whatever they do to me, I'll kill you first!" Janna did not doubt it, he looked and sounded so ferocious.

"I won't tell," she whispered.

"How do I know I can trust you?" the boy asked. "How do I know you won't run tattling to your mammy and pappy the minute I let you go?"

That was exactly what Janna had been planning to do and she didn't see how he could prevent it, for, as he had said himself, if she disappeared, her family would tear down the house to find her. Who was he, anyway?

"Why should I keep your secret?" she asked, taking courage. "I don't know you. You're not one of the van Arkels, for you're not in their picture and you don't look like them."

Notwithstanding her bad accent, the boy seemed to understand her, for he said, "I'm a friend of theirs. I've their permission to live here, which is more than you can say, I bet. I work for them."

"What work?" Janna asked. He pointed behind him, at the table. For the first time Janna was at leisure to take in her surroundings. They were in a small, hidden room. She could not see a door; it must have been closed after she fell through. There was a fold-up cot with blankets and a pillow, an empty fireplace, and a closet. In the middle stood a table and chair, all very close together in the cramped space. The window was completely covered with ivy. A shaded gooseneck lamp shone on the table, which was covered with a variety of papers. The boy must have been working there when she had come tumbling into his sanctuary. She guessed he was about Kurt's age.

Janna took a closer look at the papers. The boy did not stop her. Janna saw identification papers and food-distribution cards. The boy had been copying the official stamp on them with the help of stencils, various inks, small brushes, and a penknife. She also saw a new razor blade among his tools.

"So you're falsifying papers," said Janna. "You belong to the Dutch Resistance." She looked at him curiously. What would Herr Frosch say!

The boy shrugged his shoulders. "You could call it that. I'm just helping the van Arkels rescue innocent people from certain death. They need these identification papers and food cards to keep alive. If you betray me, all these people will either starve or be forced to give themselves up to be sent to the gas chambers of a concentration camp."

"Gas chambers?" Janna looked at the boy with horror. "You mean... they are killed?"

The boy looked sternly at her. "Do you think," he said, "that Germany is sending Jews to a nice vacation in a spa, or to pretty villages with geraniums in the windows? That's what we were told at first, though in Holland we never believed it. We got the Jewish children that were chased over the Dutch border by frantic parents and left wandering through the woods of eastern Holland with no place to go. Mrs. van Arkel and other women collected them in their cars and found homes for them. Do you think those parents thought they were being sent to pretty villages? But even in Holland we did not know the worst till last year, through Radio Orange."

"It may just be enemy propaganda..." began Janna.

The boy shook his head. "Not a hope. There is proof... much proof. Escapees smuggled photographs..." His lips quivered.

Janna felt shocked. Death for all those people in the cattle cars!

"And these papers are helping some to escape?" she asked.

The boy looked at her curiously. "You care, don't you?" he said in a warmer tone. "Funny, I didn't think any Muff cared." Janna blinked and he explained: "That's what we call the Germans, because in the old days German officers wore muffs to keep their hands warm."

"Oh," said Janna. She had never heard of that. Hitler would not have allowed it. His officers had to be tough.

"Show me what you do," she said.

"As you see, I copy stamps. It's tricky work. I would not have the patience if I did not know that each stamp saves a life."

Janna was impressed. She nodded. "I promise to keep your secret," she said. The boy gave a sigh of relief.

A trapdoor in the floor slowly opened and Mina's head stuck out. Her expression of surprise was ludicrous. Her eyebrows did not know which way to go.

"Janna!" she gasped. "What are *you* doing here?"

"I found the place," said Janna calmly, beginning to enjoy herself. "I should report this boy and you too...but I won't," she ended hastily, as Mina made a motion to throw the tray which she was carrying at her head. There was food on it, and a lot of mysteries were cleared up at once.

"You'd better not, Miss Snoop." Mina heaved herself out of the trap hole. "For if you breathe a word of this to anyone, I'll come when you are sleeping and slit your throat with my carving knife. That's a promise." She talked in a low voice, but it sounded all the more fierce.

"I won't, I won't," Janna whispered back.

"That's understood then." Mina put the tray on the table. "How did you find this place?" Janna explained again and Mina examined the blank wall. Only a very faint crack showed the outline of a door. She felt the spring catch.

"You must not have shut it properly," she told the boy. "I warned you it was dangerous. He *will* sneak out at night, to get air on your balcony," she told Janna.

So that was the breathing Janna had heard, and not Heinz at all!

"Have you been hiding here long?" she asked the boy.

"Almost two years now, isn't it, Mina?" Mina nodded, an expression of pity on her face which Janna thought misplaced. You don't pity heroes.

"I am Johanna Oster," she said, holding out her hand. "Who are you?"

"I am Sef van Gelder." They shook hands formally, as if they hadn't been glaring at each other a few moments ago. Mina's eyebrows registered approval.

"You'd better go now," she told Janna. "Lunch is ready and they'll be wondering where you are. Now, don't you go in and out of here, that's too dangerous. Remember!" And she made a movement with her finger across her throat.

"You don't have to threaten me," said Janna proudly. "I gave my word already before you popped up, didn't I, Sef?"

"You did," Sef confirmed.

"Because of his work, because he is saving lives," Janna explained.

Mina nodded at Sef. "She means it, it's all right," she said. With this unexpected compliment, she showed Janna how to work the catch of the door, which was one with a panel in Janna's wardrobe.

When Janna hurried down to lunch, Heinz intercepted her. "Where were you?" he asked. "I looked everywhere, even in your wardrobe, but you weren't there. If you went into the garden, it was no fair. You *said* the third floor…"

"I'm not going to tell you where I was," said Janna. "I want to use the place again next time."

"You cheated," said Heinz, glowering at her. "I bet you went to the attic or someplace like that!" and he stuck out his tongue at her.

Janna wondered why she had wasted sympathy on him that morning.

The Accident

JANNA WORRIED ABOUT HER SECRET. She kept noticing things that should have given it away: the amount of milk Mina took in, for instance...though Corrie's basket could account for that. Then there were extra sheets hanging on the line, and Mina's disappearances. But Janna soon found that people don't see what they don't look for. A stowaway in the house was too fantastic for anyone to suspect.

Now Janna had another worry. Her conscience began to bother her, especially when her parents were nice to her. Was it right to keep such a serious matter hidden from them? She'd always been very open with them. The ring didn't count; that was her own private make-believe. You didn't tell your parents when you didn't walk on the lines in the street, or had a bet with yourself to touch every third tree with your finger.

The trouble was, would Sef's secret be safe with them? On no account must the Frosches hear of it. That would be the end of Sef, and probably of Mina too, and the van Arkels.

One morning, when the Frosches had breakfasted early, Janna was with her parents alone at the table. Sitting there so intimately, her guilt pressed on her till she decided to confide in them.

"Papa," she began.

"Yes, dear," her father answered absently, his mind on his paper.

"Papa, there's something I must tell you..."

"Fire away then," said her father without looking up. "A little more coffee please, Mechtild..." and he gave a shove to his cup in Mechtild's direction.

"I was playing hide-and-seek with Heinz," began Janna.

"That was nice of you," said her mother. "I feel sorry for that boy. He has atrocious manners, but he lives an unnatural life with no boy of his own age to play with. I don't like the way his father treats him either..."

Otto gave an exclamation. "Listen to this," he said. "They found a Dutch Resistance worker who was making fake passports for Jews. He'll be shot, of course...but he's the father of eight children. How can anyone be so irresponsible and foolish as to risk his life for some Jews! What's going to happen to his family now?"

"But if he saved the Jews' lives?" asked Janna.

"Nonsense," said her father. "That's melodrama and propaganda. No harm is coming to the Jews. They are merely removed to a safe locality where they can live their own lives without harming anyone. They'll be made comfortable. We're Germans, not barbarians."

Janna looked at her mother, who was staring at her plate. She remembered the cattle cars, the scream in the Jewish quarter, the baby with the star...What had Hugo said about lies?...

"Well, what was it you wanted to tell me?" asked her father.

"Oh, it's not really important," said Janna. "Just something about Heinz." Her father went back to his paper.

Janna could not help thinking a lot about Sef. He was so good-looking, rather like Siegfried in her book. Sef was a hero too, risking his life to help other people. Yet he was in Janna's power. One word from her...It was a thrilling thought.

She had found a book on magic in the library. There really was such a thing. Especially in Africa, strange things could happen. Witches made little statues, and if they pricked a pin somewhere, a person far away could feel a pain in that exact place. They could kill someone that way. There were witch doctors who made charms against the witches. It was all very interesting.

Every night there was a clatter of antiaircraft guns. Janna was used to it now, she usually slept through it, but one night the noise was so loud and accompanied by explosions that she woke up and left her bed to look. It was like a fireworks display. She was standing in her bathrobe by the window, watching the battle in the sky, when a voice behind her said, "Pretty sight, isn't it?" Sef was standing beside her. His enthusiasm was not for the spectacle, she felt, but for the enemy action.

"Sef!" she whispered, alarmed. "My parents might come in here, to see if I'm all right."

"I locked the door," said Sef calmly. Then, with concern, "Oh, look, they got a British plane...poor fellows..." as an airplane hurtled from the sky, a flaming missile.

"How can I keep your secret if you act like this?" Janna scolded. "Heinz might hear us talking. He sleeps right overhead. He already thinks the house is haunted because he has heard noises."

"With this racket?" asked Sef as Janna shrank under a deafening volley of antiaircraft fire. They watched a bomb explode in a sunset of sparks, throwing a red glow over the houses. Fire engines screamed.

"Can't you understand?" Sef coaxed. "I've been cooped up for two years and I haven't talked to anyone but Mina for months. Mina is all right, she's a darling, but she's pretty old. In a way I'm glad you found me, it makes a diversion."

Janna felt a thrill. She began to realize the possibilities of having a real friend in the house, someone to talk to instead of Heinz.

"You've been in my room before, haven't you?" she asked.

"Yes," said Sef. "I climbed down from your balcony into the garden and stretched my legs...There, that was a big hit..." as a fountain of fire sprayed upward.

"I could have woken up," said Janna. "I did wake once, only I thought it was Heinz playing a trick."

"You learn to take risks," said Sef coolly, "when you live with death at your elbows all the time. If you didn't, you'd soon stop breathing for fear it would betray you. But the necessity of it makes me angry. How does anyone dare to lord it over other people's lives like that?"

Janna thought Sef was referring to the war and said, "Hitler is trying to save Europe. It is now in the same danger it was when the Teutonic Knights stopped the hordes of Genghis Khan at Liegnitz."

Sef burst into laughter. "Don't you learn history in Germany, little Muff?" he asked.

"Yes, we have history," Janna answered stiffly.

"Then you ought to know that if the Teutonic Knights stopped the hordes of Genghis Khan it must have been with their dead bodies. They were soundly beaten at Liegnitz, their leaders killed, their armies wiped out, to the relief of the Poles, who were being cruelly oppressed by them."

Janna bit her lip. Was there no end to the lies she had been told?

"Is that really true?" she asked.

"Look it up in an encyclopedia if you don't believe me," said Sef.

The bombers had drifted off; the sky was black and empty again.

"The show is over," sighed Sef. "I'm going back to my prison." He disappeared into the wardrobe and Janna went back to sleep.

The next day the papers were full of the bombing of the Carlton Hotel and the descent of the burning plane behind it. There were several dead and wounded. At breakfast Herr Frosch held forth on the wickedness of the British and his conviction that Dutch traitors had had a hand in it. How otherwise could the English have known that the Luftgau Command was in that hotel? He began to enumerate the reprehensible and dangerous doings of the Resistance forces and the necessity of punishing them. Every time he looked in Janna's direction, she blushed.

Janna had enjoyed Sef's midnight visit, but when, later, at a safe moment, she rapped at the wardrobe panel and obeyed Sef's signal to come in, she found Mina lecturing him about it.

"Young gentlemen don't invade ladies' bedrooms at night," she decreed.

"Hear counsel and receive instruction that thou mayest be wise in thy latter end!" Sef's eyes met Janna's and they laughed. With a thrill Janna realized that they were in league against Mina's narrow ideas of propriety. Janna looked around Sef's "prison." The first time she hadn't taken it all in. She noticed that the ceiling was made of thick wooden beams. She realized suddenly that Heinz's room must be above it...the part that made it larger than hers. Of course!

She realized that the clothes in the wardrobe muffled all sounds coming from the secret room. Perhaps that's why the dresses had not been brought to the attic! The wall behind the cot adjoined the home of the old ladies, and the next wall was taken up by the closet and the fireplace, which probably shared the chimney of the house with the uninteresting garden. So there were three families who might have heard unusual sounds, though Sef had of course been careful. Now they'd have to watch out, but it was hard to whisper all the time. She looked at Sef, who was squatting on the ground, all bony arms and legs. Mina had spread herself out on the bed and Janna straddled the chair. Their lowered voices gave an intimate quality to their conversation.

There were books and papers all over the little room: piled in corners or stacked on shelves. All Dutch, of course.

"Sef is a great reader," Mina told Janna. She talked Dutch to Janna now, a great compliment to Janna's progress in the language. "He never likes the books I bring him, so maybe you'd better help him." A smile lit Sef's eyes and took the sulkiness from his face. He really did look like Siegfried, Janna thought.

"Nella used to do that for me," he said. "Janna reminds me of Nella, don't you think, Mina?"

"She isn't half as pretty," said Mina loyally. "Not that you're bad-looking, Janna," she added kindly.

But Janna had the feeling that Mina resented her. It was partly fear of the danger; Janna knowing about Sef doubled the risks. But there was something else. Mina was so watchful and suspicious, Janna wondered what was worrying her. Mina insisted that Janna and Sef should see each other only with Mina's approval and supervision. Janna thought she must be jealous, wanting to keep Sef all to herself. She tried to plead with Mina.

"I'll be careful, honest. He's right next door to me...Why can't I hop in when it's safe and talk to him? It would be fun..." But Mina's mouth and eyebrows were unrelenting.

"A prudent man foreseeth evil and hideth himself, but the simple pass on and are punished," she quoted, which meant she was upset. The more she worried, the more she recited Scripture. Janna would have disobeyed her, but Sef would not allow that.

"Mina has done everything for me. She has saved my life," he said. "When the van Arkels were thrown out with only an hour to get together their belongings, they could not do anything about me. Mina stayed to look after me. It was very brave of her."

Janna accepted the fact that Sef's work was secret, but she wondered at his dependence on Mina. She felt frustrated. Sef was not the only one who had been lonely. Janna too had missed congenial companionship. Now Mina stood in the way of her finding it. She remembered her ring. Only half believing, she rubbed it, wished that Mina would stop interfering. Immediately afterward she felt guilty, she did not know why.

Janna always went up to do her room after breakfast. Corrie had more work than she could manage and Janna did not really like someone else putting things away so that she had to search for them afterward. Besides, Mina did not want Corrie to know about Sef.

"You mean, you never told her?" exclaimed Janna.

"It's too dangerous," said Mina. "Goodness knows whom she meets when she goes home every night. It's especially dangerous this time," she added, her eyebrows quirked, "for it is her month to tell the truth!"

Janna was straightening her bed when a noise made her look up. The wardrobe door was ajar and she heard Sef whisper, "Janna, come, something terrible has happened!" Janna dropped the blankets and crawled into the wardrobe, remembering to shut the doors behind her.

Once in the secret room she was grabbed by Sef, who panted, "Mina was bringing up my breakfast and she fell down the ladder. I don't know what to do! Please come!"

Janna climbed down the ladder after Sef. Mina was lying at the bottom. The tray she had been carrying lay on the ground amid broken crockery and cracked eggs.

"Oh Janna, it's *you*," sighed Mina gratefully. "Please put some sense into that boy. I think I fractured my leg, but it isn't the end of the world."

Janna felt a shock of dismay and remorse. The ring! Her wish! This was *her* fault! But she hadn't wanted that, she hadn't meant for Mina to be harmed. She knelt down. Mina's ankle was badly swollen. It hurt at a touch. Janna looked around. They were in a room she had not seen before, slightly larger than the one upstairs. It was empty except for some gymnastic apparatus hanging from the ceiling and some chairs stacked against one wall. A bathroom was visible through an open door. An ivy-covered window let in the same greenish light as in Sef's room, and another empty fireplace let in some fresh air.

"What shall we do?" asked Janna. "Is this another secret room?"

Sef nodded. "If they find her here, they'll discover everything."

"Don't stand there talking," groaned Mina. "I'm in terrible pain. You've got to get me out of here. I have to have my accident someplace else." She closed her eyes, looking so pale that Janna was afraid she'd faint, like Corrie.

"The two of us could lift you into the long room," said Sef. "But there's nothing there to fall from, except the piano..."

"Don't be an idiot," said Mina. "Janna can fetch a ladder. I had an itch to dust the ceiling... Come, get a move on."

"How do we get into the long room?" asked Janna, bewildered.

"This way," said Sef. He pointed to another door. Janna opened it cautiously and stood facing a piece of canvas. It was the back of a picture. There was a hole in one of the corners. Janna stooped and looked through it. She saw the long room with the fireplace and mirror facing her at the other end. She was behind the van Arkel picture!

The long room was empty and Sef nudged her. "Go on," he said. "Get the ladder, quick!" Janna pushed the picture away from her and slipped down a foot or so into the long room. The picture slid back behind her. Janna ran to the kitchen, where Heinz was pouring himself a glass of milk.

"Where have you been, Janna?" he asked. "Hugo is waiting for you."

"You'd better go to your own lessons," Janna answered severely. "Your mother says she'll tell your father if you don't come."

It was an invention, but it served its purpose. Wiping his mouth, Heinz ran up the stairs. Janna fetched the ladder and carried it up, making as little noise as possible. She had an excuse ready if someone caught her at it; she'd say she'd seen a spider web high up in her room. But she managed to get to the long room unobserved. She had grabbed a dustcloth from the kitchen rack and she dropped it beside the ladder. Slipping behind the picture, she joined the others. Mina looked bad. Perspiration stood in pearls on her forehead.

"You took *ages*," Sef said reproachfully. He was tenderly stroking Mina's hair.

Mina smiled at Janna. "It only seemed long to us," she said. "Get me out of here now and try not to hurt me too much..."

Janna made sure no one was about. She and Sef lifted Mina awkwardly, upset by her stifled groans. They carried her to the door, where Janna held the picture away while Sef lowered Mina as gently as possible to the floor of the long room. Then Sef retreated behind the picture. Janna straightened it. She noticed that poor Mina's underlip showed how hard she had bitten it to keep from screaming. Now Janna threw down the ladder as hard as she could. Mina gave a blood-curdling shriek. (She said afterward that it was a relief after holding it in for so long.) Janna ran into the hall crying, "Mina's had an accident...Mina's had an accident!"

The Osters had not yet left. They came running, all concern. Corrie hurried down from upstairs, still carrying a broom, followed by Frau Frosch and Heinz. Herr Frosch was on the point of leaving for work and arrived in coat and hat. Hugo wandered in from the library, holding a book.

Herr Frosch showed great solicitude, scolding Frau Oster for letting Mina do such dangerous work as dusting a ceiling.

"We could get an orderly to do that sort of thing," he said pompously. "It's inexcusable to give such a task to a *cook*." Mechtild, bewildered, scarcely knew what he was talking about. She was all concern for Mina. She immediately rang the Baron, while Herr Frosch rang Herr Rauter. Within a short time, two motorcars stood ready to convey Mina to the hospital.

When Mina had left, Janna went to her lessons. The accident weighed on her. She could not help thinking it was her fault. She had not directly wished for it, of course, but perhaps it was the only way Mina could be kept from interfering.

"Do you believe in magic?" she asked Hugo. He was looking very tired, she noticed.

"The questions you ask," he said, smiling a little. "So much depends on what you mean by magic. I don't believe in arbitrary suspension of the laws of nature, but I think there are laws we have not discovered yet, hidden powers of the mind which we have hardly tapped. Much that is called magic may be caused quite naturally."

"For instance, the magic ring of the *Nibelungen*, do you believe in that?"

"Magic in legends is often symbolic," said Hugo. "Wagner made the ring's magic generate inordinate love of power. He meant to show that this only leads to doom and destruction; but Wagner, though he called himself a Christian, was a German too, and according to Heine, who was one himself, all Germans have a suppressed longing for violence. Heine warned that one day the thin layer of Germany's civilization would crack and that Germany's tribal hordes would then erupt like lava, to the horror and destruction of Europe. Wagner unconsciously, I think, gloried in the holocaust at the end of his operas. That's what gives them their compelling quality and their attraction for people like Hitler. There's a primitive satisfaction in destruction and bloodshed for its own sake."

It wasn't at all what Janna had wanted to hear. "I only meant...is there *ordinary* magic?" she said desperately. "Could you wish somebody just... to go away a little, and then she has an accident?"

Hugo looked at her thoughtfully. "Unfortunately, I do think it possible," he said, "but only if the wishing person has a powerful purpose and occult powers. These exist, I know, but shouldn't be meddled with."

When her lessons were over, Janna hurried to her bedroom, where she finished making her bed. Then she tapped on the panel door.

"Come in," Sef said. "What kept you? I was worried sick." His hair was ruffled and there was a strained look on his face. Janna realized that she had been thoughtless. She had left Sef in suspense. She told him that there had been a message from the hospital that Mina's leg had been set and that she was resting comfortably.

Sef groaned and ran his fingers through his hair. "Oh, what shall I do?"

"I'll look after you," said Janna.

"That's not the only thing. I've finished my cards and they should go off as soon as possible. People are waiting for them. Mina always looked after it for me."

"Can I help?" asked Janna.

Sef smiled. "No, little Muff," he said. "Good as you've been, we can't trust you with the secrets of our organization." Janna blushed. She hadn't thought of that. She'd be an underground worker herself then.

"I suppose you did not clean up the mess downstairs," she said.

"No, should I have?" Sef was taken back.

"We'd better do it; someone might miss the tray. I'll have to take the blame for the broken crockery, I suppose."

"I hardly think I can," said Sef wryly.

They found the mess just as they'd left it, except that the eggs had congealed into rubbery disks. Janna got a broom and gently swept the broken shards together on a piece of newspaper while Sef did exercises on the gymnastic apparatus.

"The van Arkels gave me that," he said, doing a somersault on the rings. "They thought my muscles might get weak otherwise." Janna leaned on her broom.

"Was this their gymnasium?" she asked. "Why was it hidden?"

"It used to be a Roman Catholic chapel," said Sef. "When this house was built, we had just freed ourselves from Catholic Spain and we'd outlawed all Catholic religious ceremonies. Priests had to disguise themselves as window cleaners or chimney sweeps and sneak into warehouses to say Mass among packing cases. Rich Catholics built hidden chapels in their homes and this was one of them. I'm sleeping in what was called a priest's hole. Look!" He went to the end of the room and pushed against the wall. Miraculously it receded and a tiny little altar of brown varnished wood swung toward them and clicked into place. It was a totally undistinguished little altar, but Janna stared at it with widening eyes. For there, hanging over it in a heavy, ornate frame, hung the most beautiful little picture she had ever seen. It glowed in warm tints of brown and copper, representing the inside of a church. A priest in glittering vestments bent over a baby, held by its mother, the husband slightly lost in the shadows. All the light, all the golden glow, hung about the baby...Janna gave a stifled cry... *the Rembrandt!*

Janna Helps Out

"What's the matter?" asked Sef. He had pulled out one of the chairs and was sitting astride it. He looked at Janna through strands of russet hair. Behind him the whitewashed wall was full of cracks and scribbles. The greenish light made everything a bit spooky.

"I think that's the painting my mother has been searching for," she said.

"It's a Rembrandt," Sef told her. "It's the most valuable thing the van Arkels own. It's been in the family for generations."

"Hitler wants it," said Janna. "My parents will be punished if they don't hand it over. They're suspected of stealing it, as if they were thieves!"

Sef rocked his chair with his long legs. There was an odd expression on his face.

"What else do you call it," he drawled, "when someone enters a country uninvited and without warning, after having signed a non-aggression pact, and then kicks its citizens out of their homes without giving them an opportunity to collect their possessions? Have you another name for it?"

"That's not my parents' fault," Janna spat back. "They had nothing to do with it. They only wanted somewhere to live where they could have me. I'd been away for over two years. It was the army that did it."

"That does not prevent your parents from enjoying the spoils, does it?"

"They have no other place to go," said Janna, near tears. "And they don't want the picture. My mother said at first not to give it. But Hitler needs it for his museum and so…"

"So he must have it. He must always have what he fancies, whether it's right or wrong," Sef said softly. "Whether it's countries, or art, or a million helpless souls, he must have it served for his breakfast, mustn't he?"

Janna blushed and stamped her foot. "You don't understand," she cried. "He is our *ruler*."

Sef laid his hand warningly across her mouth. "Hush, this place isn't as soundproof as upstairs," he whispered. Then he went on, "More shame that he is your ruler. Can't you see he is an ogre?"

Janna stood with downcast eyes. "I must have that picture," she insisted. "I don't want my parents put in prison. I'm going to tell my mother about it."

"So?" said Sef. "And will you tell her where you found it, so you can serve Mina, the van Arkels, and me to your ogre?"

"Oh dear," sighed Janna. "I wish Mina were here. She'd know what to do."

"Why not wait till she comes back?" asked Sef. "There isn't that much of a hurry, is there?" He pressed a corner of the altar and it pivoted around silently, with its precious load, leaving a blank wall.

"Come on upstairs," said Sef. In his own little room he began sorting out his finished work. Janna watched him. She noticed how deftly and surely his long fingers handled the documents.

"You're clever," she said. "I can't see which are your stamps and which are the originals."

"I wish it were true," sighed Sef. "A microscope would show the difference at once, but it won't come to that unless the Germans become suspicious."

"How did you get into this?" asked Janna, suddenly worried. It seemed frightfully dangerous work.

Sef straightened and stretched himself. His hands almost touched the ceiling. "I was studying to become a sculptor," he said. "Every Saturday afternoon I went to this famous Amsterdam sculptor for lessons. When the racial persecutions began in '41, he started on these forgeries. His pupils were the first ones to help him. I'm only one in an assembly line. I do these particular stamps, but there are many others. One for each district. There are also signatures to be forged and a watermark which has to be simulated. That's very delicate work…a girl does it."

"How do you get the models?"

"Oh, we have patriots in the offices who smuggle them out."

"I thought you said you worked for the van Arkels?"

"Well, they're in it too."

"Can't the Jews get food without these papers?" asked Janna, shivering a little. She realized that it would matter very much to her if something happened to Sef.

"How could they? Everything is rationed. The shops have barely enough to honor the coupons. The only other way is the Black Market and few Jews are rich enough for that."

"How many people are there in hiding?" asked Janna.

"Over two hundred thousand, I should imagine," said Sef. "They are not all Jews. We have students hiding because they did not sign the oath of loyalty and others to escape the labor draft. Then there are our illegal workers, our Knuckle gangs, who do the sabotage. They're on the run all the time. The only place to hide here is in other people's houses. We have no forests or mountains."

"And you have to feed them all?"

"Our group? No, of course not. We take care of a limited number. There are other groups doing the same thing, all over the country." Sef went on sorting and wrapping the documents.

"What happens if Hitler wins the war?" asked Janna.

"Don't worry about that," said Sef. "It won't happen."

"But *if*," persisted Janna.

"Then," said Sef, looking at her with wide-open hazel eyes, "then all our work is for nothing. We'll all be killed and the killing will go on for a long time, because your ogre lives on blood."

"But he said..." faltered Janna.

"I'll tell you what he said," interrupted Sef. "He said that lies were the greatest weapon of a ruler, and the bigger the lie, the more readily it is believed."

"So...so..." began Janna again.

"So you can believe on his own authority that everything he said has been a lie." Janna felt uneasy. This was a little too radical for her.

"I...I think I'd better go..." she said. "Mina being away, they may need my help."

"Yes, little Muff," said Sef. "You'd better go and think over what I've told you."

Janna took the tray with the shards and the mess wrapped in newspaper with her, as well as the broom. She disposed of them tidily in the kitchen. To the surprised Corrie she explained that she and Heinz had wanted to have a party but she had accidentally dropped the tray. Corrie accepted her explanation placidly. Janna liked her but sometimes suspected that she wasn't very bright.

Lunch was a sketchy affair of biscuits and weak tea. Herr Frosch grumbled his way through, going on and on about the hazards of cooks dusting ceilings. Everyone longed for a hot meal, but there was no one to cook it. The household was in utter confusion. Corrie, so quick and capable under Mina's direction, now rushed around like a headless chicken, starting on one thing and leaving it for another. Mounds of dust lay on the floor beside an abandoned broom, silverware was left soaking in the sink while wrinkled clothing languished beside a cooling iron. Frau Oster, who had an exceptionally difficult part to rehearse, felt distracted. She hadn't been able to find a substitute for Mina. The hospital had advised her that Mina would have to stay there for a while. The prospect of eating out of cans loomed threateningly.

"Oh dear," said Janna's mother. "I wish there was someone in the house who could cook. Frau Frosch is useless. When I asked her if she could boil an egg, she wanted to know whether you used water or milk!"

"I can cook," said Janna. She might have dropped a bombshell, her mother looked so surprised.

"Didn't you read my letters?" asked Janna. "I told you Frau Kopp often made me cook her meals. As long as it's not complicated and I don't have to kill chickens..." she stipulated.

"Kill chickens!" Her mother shuddered. "You don't mean to tell me they made you kill chickens?"

"Mother, I wrote you. We had all sorts of things to do for those farmers: clear out manure, currycomb horses, feed pigs..."

"Heavens!" cried her mother. "And did Erna allow that?"

"Erna had nothing to do with it. It was the law. We were obliged to help on the land. Didn't you know that?"

"You said something...but I thought it was for rural children..." Her mother's voice trailed off as she realized that she had not thought about it at all. "Well, it's a good thing you learned to cook," she said, cheering up, "because I don't know the difference between a turnip and a potato. I'll leave the kitchen to you then. I've got to go." With a relieved smile she left.

And so, quite casually, Janna was made free in Mina's kingdom. She could poke about there to her heart's content and she found all sorts of interesting things...a little cellar where coal and potatoes and cabbages were kept and where Mina had hidden a perfectly good bicycle! She also found an unused stove in a corner of the kitchen which she had not noticed before. She realized that these were the only places in the house she and her mother hadn't ransacked for the painting. They hadn't dared to!

She also noticed that the supplies in the house were rather unbalanced. Corrie explained that it all depended on what the Baron had been able to get hold of. There was a larder full of Russian caviar, there were cartons full of pickles, boxes full of oyster crackers, and some vegetables in cans. On the other hand, though there was a sack of flour, there was no bread, and Janna didn't know how to make any. They were out of butter and milk, and the only fresh vegetable was cabbage.

Janna finally opened a can of mushrooms and made soup with them. She boiled some potatoes and made a salad out of cabbage leaves. Then she used some leftover porridge and made fried cakes with it.

"Why doesn't the Baron send us more sensible food?" she asked peevishly. "Who wants caviar?"

"You could serve it on oyster crackers," suggested Corrie. "You should not complain, you're well off. Many people are eating bulbs."

"Tulip bulbs?" asked Janna. "Can you eat those?"

"At certain times of the year," said Corrie. "At other times they're poisonous. You don't know how lucky you are."

A little ashamed, Janna went on preparing the dinner. It wasn't too bad, though Herr Frosch looked gloomy. He made his whole meal out of caviar.

Corrie stayed late to help with the dishes. Afterward Janna was faced with carrying up Sef's dinner. How to do that without being detected? Her admiration for Mina increased.

After Corrie had left, she looked about for a way to disguise the tray. She found a deep clothes basket in which it fitted. She draped newly ironed garments over the basket and cautiously mounted the stairs. Mina had always gone through the long room but Janna preferred to use her wardrobe. She did not think she could manage the ladder.

Her mother saw her and said, "Now really, Janna, you don't have to do that...Let Corrie carry up the ironing."

"Yes, Mother," said Janna, hastily disappearing into her room and wondering how Mina had done it.

It was disappointing after all the trouble not to find Sef in his room. Perhaps he was in the chapel. She descended the ladder and looked around, she even peeped into the toilet, but he wasn't there. Where could he be? She climbed the ladder again. No, he wasn't hiding for a joke. She did not see him in his closet or under his bedclothes. Then she noticed that the table looked bare. The finished work was gone. Sef had left! He had risked going into the streets to deliver it. She remembered the skinny boy the SS had tried to arrest, thinking he was of age. Would they not think it far more of tall, stalwart Sef, with his manly voice? And if they arrested him, they would find the forged papers...Janna groaned. She sat on Sef's bed and buried her face in her hands. It was all her fault. Why, oh why had she made that stupid wish? She paced up and down the little room, her hands squeezed together, knowing there was no one she could go to for advice. She was left alone with the whole responsibility of Sef, with the secret...and she was afraid to use the ring again. At last she crawled into bed. As she turned down her blankets, she found a note on her pillow.

"Gone out—back soon," it said. It was risky, foolish, unnecessary...but it warmed her heart. With the note in her hand she fell asleep.

Troubles

When Janna opened her eyes the next morning, she knew something extraordinary had happened. Then she saw Sef's piece of paper and it all came back to her. She destroyed the paper (Heinz must not find it) and went to the wardrobe, half hoping Sef had come back in the night. She'd left the window open. But the room was just as it had been the day before. The bed had not been slept in. She knew it was no use looking in the chapel...he hadn't come back. Meanwhile, the household depended on her for its food. She dressed hurriedly and ran downstairs to the kitchen. Heinz was already banging about there and Janna began to understand Mina's dislike of children in the kitchen.

"When are you going to make breakfast?" whined Heinz. "I'm hungry!"

"It's not that late," said Janna, looking at the kitchen clock. "Leave me to it, will you?"

"No, I've just as much right to be here as you," said Heinz. "I'll help you." Luckily Corrie came in with an empty tray.

"Oh no, you don't," she said with deep feeling. "You march right out of here." A mollified Heinz departed.

"Thanks, Corrie," said Janna.

"That boy," grumbled Corrie. "If I have to tell the truth, I'm glad there are only girls in our family. A brother like that would have driven me mad."

Janna made coffee and fresh porridge. She piled more caviar on oyster biscuits. Herr Frosh ate the caviar but refused the porridge, and then grumbled at the monotony of his diet.

As Janna was washing up afterward, she could not get Sef out of her mind.

"Corrie, when a boy looks the right age and is walking the streets, do the police always pick him up?"

"Mostly," said Corrie. "Of course, if he doesn't meet an official, he might get away with it. But it's a risk hardly anyone would dare take. When they are caught they are punished, you see. They're supposed to give themselves up."

"What if they are carrying something forbidden, like forged papers?"

"Oh my goodness," cried Corrie. "They'd be finished then!" Corrie was talking quite naturally to Janna. Sometimes Janna thought she forgot that Janna was German.

A sick feeling spread upward from Janna's stomach. She almost lost her breakfast. When Hugo arrived that day, he seemed to echo her mood. He looked more ill and spent than usual. Janna told him to sit down, she'd get him some coffee and something to eat, but he stopped her.

"I couldn't swallow a bite," he said, sinking into his chair and covering his face with his hands. "My best friend and his wife were arrested in the night, with their little daughters. Police banging on the door...they had hardly time to put on their coats. I heard it all from the neighbors."

"Oh dear," said Janna, thinking of Sef. "Why were they taken?"

"For the crime of being Jewish, for breathing when they're not supposed to exist. I offered to hide them long ago. I begged them to share my flat. Rachel was willing—she was thinking of the babies—but Saul would not hear of it. He did not want to endanger me. 'As if that matters,' I said. 'What's my life worth? I, a hunchback, with no prospect of a normal life...why can't I risk it for you? I'd be glad to.' But he would not listen. I think he had a religious reason. He seemed to think the persecution was sent by God for a mysterious purpose.

"'We must not refuse it,' he said. 'God will give us the strength to bear whatever happens. It's also for you Christians that we suffer.' I'll never forget his face when he said that. I never knew a finer man. He gave Rachel the courage to face up to it too."

Janna sat very still. She hardly recognized her cool, detached teacher. At last Hugo looked up.

"Sorry, Janna, I should not worry you about this." Then, surprised, he said, "I talk to you like a friend, don't I? I have a confession to make. I hated to take this job, but I had to, I was starving. I've come to enjoy it. It's a pleasure teaching a sensitive, honest child."

Janna blushed. "It's been wonderful for me too," she said. "I feel as if I were lost in a jungle and you cut a path for me."

"You did a lot of it yourself," said Hugo. "You've restored some of my faith in human nature. I always believed that there was a compass in the human breast forever pointing to what's true and good... or, to make another comparison, that like a root or bulb we cannot be so deeply buried or a green shoot will break its way through to the light. You've proved it, my dear, you've proved it, putting older people to shame." They smiled at each other.

"I think it's...it's because lies don't *fit*," said Janna. "Something keeps sticking out."

Hugo laughed. "Very well put," he said. "Where were we with our geometry last time...?"

After the lesson Janna ran up to her room to see whether Sef had arrived, but he was still missing. She felt desperate. She longed for Mina. If only she had someone to talk things over with! She hated to do it... things might go wrong again, but she rubbed her ring and wished Mina back. It worked! That very day Mina returned in an ambulance. She had refused to stay in the hospital. Janna's parents were out but she and Corrie settled Mina in her room, after the ambulance men had carried her up five flights of stairs.

As soon as Corrie had left, Mina fixed Janna with a gimlet stare and said, "What have you and Sef been up to? Out with it!"

Janna burst into tears. "We haven't been up to anything... He's gone..." she sobbed.

"Gone!" Mina hadn't looked exactly rosy, but now she became paler still. "You don't mean..."

"No, no," Janna hastened to assure her. "It's not as bad as that. At least, I hope it isn't. He... he went to deliver his finished work."

"The fool!" spluttered Mina. "That's what I was afraid of. That's why I insisted they bring me home. Not that I wanted to stay there, the food they served would not have filled a hollow tooth... Why didn't you stop him from going?" she asked suddenly, lifting threatening eyebrows at Janna.

"He didn't tell me," faltered Janna. "He... he was gone when I brought him his dinner."

"Ah!" said Mina. "At least he waited till dark. He won't come back in broad daylight either; he's not that kind of an idiot. He may have stayed with a friend... he'll have enjoyed that. Poor boy, he's been cooped up for so long."

"You don't think the police will get him?" asked Janna with quivering lips.

"Why think the worst? As the Good Book says, 'Hope maketh not ashamed.' If we didn't trust in a loving providence, how could we get through these days? What I'd like now, my dear, is a nice hot cup of the Baron's tea. What they served in the hospital was bilge water."

Janna went downstairs, greatly relieved to have laid her burden on Mina's broad shoulders.

It had been raining all that day. Her father was suffering from an attack of bronchitis and had gone to bed early with aspirin and a sleeping pill. His understudy had to take over that night.

Janna went to bed early too but could not get to sleep. She was worrying about Sef out in that bad weather. It must have been close to curfew time when she heard the french windows open gently. She whispered, "Is that you, Sef?"

"Yes," he whispered back, shutting the blackout drapes behind him. Janna switched on her bed light and smothered a laugh. Sef was dripping wet and enveloped in a huge old-fashioned cape with a hood that covered most of his face. He threw it off.

"Brrr, what a day," he said, putting down the package he was carrying.

"Didn't you deliver your work?" Janna asked anxiously.

"Yes, I did. I delivered the documents and got some more to do. Guess what! I've been to see Nella." He had taken a chair and was removing his wet boots.

"You saw Nella?" Janna was taken aback.

"Yes, I heard from friends that she and Eylard, her two-year-old brother, are staying here in the city with an uncle and aunt. Nella has to go on with her schooling. She just entered the Montessori Lyceum, the best high school in Amsterdam; I wish I'd been able to go there. And of course the baby has to be looked after. But she doesn't know where her parents and brothers are. They said goodbye to her and she hasn't heard from them since. Of course, they may be hiding. The boys are getting to the age where they can be picked up for labor...or they may have been arrested. She is very brave about it."

Janna blushed. So that lovely, united family was dispersed because her mother had wanted the Osters to be together!

"The uncle put me up last night," Sef went on. "He has a very knobbly sofa. Nella and I talked until late. Nella sends you her thanks for looking after me. I talked to her about the Rembrandt picture, but she said possessions did not matter where lives were at stake, so you can do what you like."

"How nice of her," said Janna, tears filling her eyes. "Couldn't we give some of her things back to her...some of her clothes? I have them in my wardrobe."

Sef smiled. "They wouldn't fit her," he said. "She's grown a lot since I saw her last. Her aunt has made her some dresses from spare things of her own. She looked all right."

"How did you escape the police?" asked Janna.

"I didn't meet any...God looked after me."

"An SS man I know says there is no God, or the SS wouldn't be here."

"Hah!" said Sef. "That's arrogance for you, making the existence of Almighty God depend on little twerps like himself."

"You must be starved," said Janna. "I'll go down and get you something."

"You speak a true word," said Sef. "I've been so well fed here I did not want to take what little they had, so I'm hollow. I dreamed all night of Mina's pancakes..."

"I don't have Mina's pancakes for you," said Janna. "I'm doing the cooking."

"You?" Sef smiled. "How is Mina?"

"Back," said Janna. "She insisted on leaving the hospital."

"Good for her," said Sef. "Was she mad I went?"

"What do you think?" asked Janna. They both laughed.

"Lock the door after me," said Janna. "I'll knock three times softly when I come back." She went out. As she passed her father's door, she heard him snoring, so the pill had worked. She went upstairs to Mina's room first, to tell her Sef was back. She thought Mina would be sleepless too, worrying about the boy. She was right. Light showed through the cracks of Mina's door. Mina said, "Come in," when Janna knocked.

"Praise be to God from Whom all blessings flow," she exclaimed when Janna told her the news. "Now I can sleep. Did he say anything?"

"Yes, he's seen Nella."

"Nella?" Mina sat upright, revealing a flannel nightgown. Janna repeated to her what Sef had said. "I'm getting him some food now," she said. "You go to sleep." She fluffed up Mina's pillow and tucked the blankets around her. "Is your leg paining you?" she asked.

"A little...it doesn't matter. You're a good child..." Mina muttered drowsily. On the way back Janna heard her father snore again. She went to the kitchen and prepared hot cocoa, fried potatoes, and crackers with caviar. She was carrying the tray upstairs when she heard a muffled cry from the library. She recognized her mother's voice. Right after that she heard the Baron say something. Her mother and the Baron were alone in the library while her father was sleeping upstairs. It made Janna grow cold inside. Without reflection Janna rubbed her ring hard and wished the Baron out of their lives...

She had hardly finished her wish when she shrank back into the shadow of one of the valuable statues. The library door had opened and the Baron strode out, looking angry.

"If that's what you think of me," he whispered hoarsely, "I'll have nothing more to do with you. I am offering you marriage, I want to make you baroness of my castle—and you call it an insult!" Her mother had followed him out, looking every bit as angry as the Baron.

"I'm a married woman," she whispered in concentrated fury. "Is it not an insult to think I'd make light of my vows?"

The Baron turned a face to her twisted with conflicting passions. "Mechtild..." he said. It was a cry of pain.

"No, Dietrich, we must not see each other again," murmured Mechtild. "You've spoiled a beautiful friendship..." she ended brokenly.

The Baron left, his cloak swirling after him so that it got caught in the door and Mechtild had to open it to release him.

Janna stood frozen, not daring to move. She saw her mother rush into the library and heard sounds of wild weeping.

Oh dear, thought Janna as she trudged upstairs with her tray. What have I done! When she arrived at the third floor, her father poked a sleepy face around the bedroom door.

"What's the noise?" he asked thickly. "Was that the front door? Where's your mother?"

"In the kitchen," Janna lied quickly. "We were making a snack. I'm eating mine in my room. Go back to sleep." Her father looked as if there was nothing he'd like better. He withdrew his head and she could hear the springs creak as he went back to his bed.

Janna gave three soft knocks on the door and Sef opened it.

"What happened?" he asked. "You were so long!" He'd been reading Janna's *Nibelungen* book. She could see it lying open on the bed.

"Hush!" she said. She listened at the door; she could hear her mother's footsteps coming up the stairs. Then her parents' bedroom door opened and closed.

"What's the matter?" Sef whispered nervously.

"She's back," said Janna.

"Who?"

"My mother, in her room."

"Where was she then? Did she see you? Has she found out about me?"

"No," said Janna. "She didn't see me. I'm afraid your cocoa is cold," she added.

"Never mind, I'll have it anyway," said Sef. "What happened? You look like a ghost."

"Nothing—at least, nothing about you. I'd rather not talk about it," said Janna.

"All right, Janneke, I won't pry," said Sef cheerfully, gobbling up his fried potatoes.

"What's that?" he asked, pointing to the caviar. Janna told him. Sef said he'd never tasted any.

"Mina must have been holding back on you. The place is full of it," Janna said, smiling. Sef tasted it but said it was too salty for him. He ate the crackers, though. His hair was still wet and clung tightly to his head.

"What did you call me just now?" asked Janna, smiling.

"Janneke, that's a Dutch diminutive of Janna. We have a song about you:

> *"Hupsa Janneke*
> *Stroop in't kanneke*
> *Laat the poppekes dansen!"*

"That means: *'Hupsa Janneke*, syrup in the jug, let the puppets dance,'" translated Janna. "Does it mean anything?"

"Oh, it's probably got some gruesome historical meaning, like most nursery rhymes," said Sef.

"You're cheering me up, Sef. I felt awful."

"I saw it," said Sef. "I've been reading that book of yours. I think Brunhilde is the only decent character in it."

"She caused Siegfried's death," Janna pointed out.

"That mutt," grumbled Sef.

"Oh no," protested Janna. "He's a hero, I love him. You're rather like him," she added shyly.

"Me? A Nordic sap like him? God forbid," said Sef. "I don't believe in that magic potion, you know. That was just a cover-up, because he was unfaithful to Brunhilde. She had a right to avenge herself. Except for her, the whole lot are crooked, Wotan most of all, the double-dealing tyrant. As for the ring, I don't think it was magic at all. They only thought it was. The curse came through their own violence, greed, and hatred."

Sef had finished his meal. Gathering up his cloak and boots and the package, he vanished into the wardrobe.

Janna put out the light and lay staring into the darkness. Her mother and the Baron…her mother's tears…had she done wrong?

Betrayal

Now began an arduous time for Janna. She and Corrie had to look after the whole household, including Mina up five flights of stairs. The advantage was that Janna did not have to disguise Sef's trays. Whenever she was seen, she blandly pretended they were for Mina. Frau Oster exclaimed over Mina's appetite!

Mechtild was wan and listless these days. The spring seemed to have gone out of her. The Baron did not come any more and even Janna missed him. Something of warmth and refinement had gone from the house.

But though the Baron stayed away, his gifts kept coming. Janna surprised her mother weeping over a brace of pheasants one day that had just been delivered. Janna tiptoed off guiltily, wondering whether she had had the right to interfere with her mother's friendship. But she had her own troubles. Nella haunted her. On one hand she felt sorry for her, without her parents, not knowing where they were...but she did not like Sef's interest in her. She was so beautiful...and she had known Sef for years. Sef must love her. Janna felt she could not bear it. Sef was her discovery, her Siegfried. She did not want to share him with Nella, even though Nella knew him first. It all came to a head one morning as she brought in Sef's lunch. She almost dropped the tray when she saw what he was doing. He was taping a photograph of Nella on the wall above his bed.

"Doesn't she look nice?" he asked, stepping away from it to judge the effect. "She gave it to me the other night."

"Did she," said Janna coldly.

"Don't you like it?" asked Sef, turning around to look at her.

"Does it matter whether I do?" asked Janna.

"Of course." Sef was grinning at her. "I've taped it up to please you. You admire her, don't you?"

"That's not true. You did it to please yourself," Janna retorted. "What do you want with me when you have Nella? Why bother with me at all?"

"Because you're around and she isn't. Anyway, the more the merrier, don't you think?" Sef looked at her in such an irritating way that Janna lost her temper.

"No," she said angrily, slamming the tray on his bed. "I hate being one of a crowd, being a stopgap. You can *have* Nella. If Mina wasn't ill, I'd never, never see you again."

"Ah!" said Sef, who seemed vastly amused. "That would be a pity. I should miss you, Janna." He was leaning with his back against the wall and looked triumphant.

"You...you..." Janna did not know what word to use to express her fury. Then a word from an old-fashioned novel came to her mind. "You... *trifler*..." She spat at him, like an angry cat, and turning, she stumbled through the wardrobe, followed by Sef's soft, teasing laughter. When she stepped into her room, she saw Heinz there, rummaging through her desk. She thought she had locked the door! Heinz looked up.

"I know what you're doing in there," he said craftily.

"Oh you do, do you..." Janna was still too angry to think. "I suppose you've found out I've a boy friend in there, haven't you?" It was out before she could help herself. When she realized what she had done, she felt sick all over. She'd betrayed Sef! Now Heinz would go looking for him, and if you searched well, you were bound to find the catch and the way into Sef's room. She felt like tearing her hair.

Heinz laughed. "You think you can fool me! That wardrobe isn't big enough. You can't fob me off. You've a radio in there and you're listening to a forbidden station!"

He hadn't believed her! Relief made Janna giddy. Then she realized what Heinz was saying. She must not contradict him; it was better he should believe that than the truth.

"You think you're smart, eh?" she jeered. "Where would I get a radio?"

"How do I know," said Heinz, shrugging his shoulders. "Perhaps you found one in the attic."

"We Germans are allowed radios, aren't we?"

"We're not allowed to listen to enemy propaganda," said Heinz. "If I tell my father..."

"Then I'll tell about the statue," Janna said promptly. She saw that had had an effect.

"Well," Heinz conceded, "maybe I won't tell. But then you must let me listen too..." He made a movement toward the wardrobe. Janna blocked his way.

"All right," she said glibly, wondering how she was going to do that. Then she asked sternly, "How did you get into my room? I know I locked the door."

"My key fits your lock," said Heinz, grinning evilly. Janna shuddered at the thought of how unsafe she had been all the times she had felt so secure!

As soon as she had got rid of Heinz, she ran up to Mina to confess what had happened. Mina was wearing a knitted bed jacket and her graying hair hung down in plaits. To Janna's surprise, she took the account fairly calmly.

"Is that all you said?" she asked, with a curious expression on her face. "That you had a boy friend in the wardrobe?"

"I said, 'In there.' Heinz thought I meant the wardrobe."

"It's a good thing he didn't believe you, though I must say, it does not sound believable. If he pesters you about the radio, you can let him listen to mine."

"Do you have one?"

"Of course. If you lift up the third floorboard, you'll find it. But it's more important to be able to lock your door. Listen..." and Mina gave Janna instructions on where to find a hook and eye to put on her door.

"And make it fit properly." she warned. "Don't leave a crack, so he can slip a knife through and lift the hook. Next time remember that 'he that is slow to anger is better than the mighty; and he that ruleth his spirit better than he that taketh a city.'" Janna hung her head.

"I promise," she said.

"Well, hurry and put up that hook and eye then," said Mina.

On the twenty-ninth of April, 1943, the Wehrmacht Befehlshaber of the Netherlands ordered that the demobilized members of the Dutch Army were to be taken into custody. They would be summoned personally in the newspapers and those who tried to escape could expect the severest retaliation. Announcements to that effect were posted all over the city. The order caused a storm of protest, just as occurred in '41, at the time of the first deportations of the Jews. A general strike broke out spontaneously all over Holland. Herr Frosch noticed first that he could not use the telephone. Then the power failed. Frau Oster had to bring out old-fashioned kerosene lamps. The next morning there was no mail. Janna served canned milk and crackers for breakfast.

"Those stupid Dutch," fumed Herr Frosch. "How do they hope to get away with it? And Seyss-Inquart is in Berchtesgaden! Herr Rauter will have to manage everything."

But Seyss-Inquart was speedily summoned. He was on his way back, bringing more Gestapo and SS troops.

Martial law was declared. There were many executions, of strikers, of prominent Dutchmen. Sef said he feared for the van Arkels, and Janna scanned the lists of victims every day, but so far the van Arkels were not among them.

Heinz had forgotten about the radio. His ambition now was to trap a Dutch officer who had failed to give himself up, and he sat for hours in his spy hole like a cat waiting for a mouse. Janna guessed that his secret wish was to wring praise out of an unappreciative father.

She herself was anxious now to have the Rembrandt safely in her parents' hands. The responsibility of keeping it hidden weighed on her. She discussed it with Mina. At first Mina had vigorously opposed her giving up the family treasure, but when Janna told her what Nella had said, she gave way.

"We'll have to stage a fake discovery, the way we had a fake accident," she said. "Let me think about it."

The theaters were closed. For the first time, as long as Janna could remember, she had her parents' company in the evenings. (Their Monday holidays did not count, for then they had social engagements.)

"Can we sit around the table like a real family?" asked Janna.

"What do you mean, minx, a real family? Aren't we real?" asked her father, pinching her cheek.

"Not like the van Arkels," said Janna.

"What do you know about the van Arkels?" asked her father, frowning.

"I know their picture," said Janna. Her mother understood.

"Let's play a game together, Otto," she said. "We can sit in the library."

Janna found a game in the recreation room, one of those where you throw dice and move little figures along numbered squares. The first player to arrive at a hundred wins the jackpot. Some squares had pictures with special meanings. Janna found some *pfeffernuesse* in a tin: tiny round spicy cookies. They would serve for the jackpot. She sat down with her parents at Hugo's table. Corrie had made up a fire in the fireplace and Janna's father lit it. It was nice to sit in the familiar room with the light of a kerosene lamp shining on the table while the fire spat and crackled, the draperies closed firmly against the outside world with its dangers. Janna sat between her parents. At last they were a loving family! She glowed.

Unfortunately her parents hadn't played long before they began to argue.

"I'm fed up with this country," her father was grumbling. "All this violence, no decent regard for law and order. It's perfectly reasonable for us to intern the army again, with a probable English invasion in the offing. All this irresponsible striking only makes things worse." He threw the dice so wildly that one of them rolled off the table. Janna picked it up.

"Two sixes, that means twelve," she said, moving her father's blue figure up twelve points. "Oh, you landed in the grave! Now you're dead, you'll have to wait till someone rescues you."

"That's exactly the way I *feel*," said her father. "It's not only the Dutch, though a colder, unfriendlier people it would be hard to find. But there is that Frosch, suspecting us of stealing the picture! I bet he told his boss, Rauter, about it. The last thing I want is to fall into the hands of the SD. I don't like their methods. Mechtild, I want to accept that invitation we received to play in Paris."

Frau Oster was advancing her yellow figure. "Dear me," she said. "I've got to go back to the beginning."

"Please do," said her husband. "Let's start over again somewhere else, Mechtild. The three of us."

"You must be joking," said Mechtild. "How do you know we'd get permission? We're appreciated here. There now, Janna, you're going to win! You got to ninety-nine."

"Oh no," said Janna. "You can't throw one with two dice. I'll have to move back again."

"I'm not joking," said Herr Oster. "No, Janna, I've got to skip my turn, don't you remember? Of course we'll get permission. It's the same sort of job, but the French are more civilized. Why should we not pull up our stakes here? We don't want to overstay our welcome."

"Twelve," said Janna's mother. "Oh, look, I can advance more, I got a bonus! I'll catch up with you yet, Janna. You forget, Otto, that we have a house here and can have Janna with us. It was hard enough to get."

"There are houses in Paris," said Herr Oster. "I have friends there, don't forget. I come from Alsace. Ah, poor Janna, you threw too much. Now you're back to eighty-nine."

"Why do you want to upset the present arrangement? We're taken care of here. The Baron sends us food." Mechtild's voice trembled a little. "There now, I'm in prison. I've got to skip a turn."

"You may land in prison if you stay here, Mechtild," warned her husband. "There is a Dutch proverb that says it's bad luck eating cherries with high-placed gentlemen."

"If you mean the Baron, you know he is not coming any more," Mechtild reminded him gently.

"I suppose he's found another man's wife's shoulder to weep on," Otto remarked unfeelingly.

"There now, Janna, you've won," said Mechtild. "All the *pfeffernuesse* are yours. No, thank you, dear, it's too soon after dinner. And a good dinner it was, even if you had to use canned food. Do you know what Mina said to me? She said you had a real talent for cooking."

"Did she?" Janna blushed with pleasure. Mina's compliments were rare.

"She did. Otto, remember, the devil you know is better than the devil you don't know."

"We may not continue to do well here," predicted her husband gloomily. "They may arrest us about that picture. Frankly, I'm scared. I wish you'd listen to me."

"If we run away now," said Mechtild, "everyone is sure to think we're guilty."

"It's the Baron," said her husband bitterly. "You don't want to leave him." He left abruptly, slamming the door.

Janna stared wide-eyed at her mother. "Do you love the Baron?" she asked.

Her mother laughed the tinkling laugh she reserved for her best roles. "Don't let your father affect you," she said. "The Baron and I are just friends…" But there was a misty look about her eyes as they stared into the distance.

Hugo

On Monday the strike was still on and Janna wondered whether Hugo would come to teach her. Some people were still going about their business, but the streets were dangerous. Janna and Heinz were not allowed outside; they had to take their exercise in the garden.

Heinz said it was a matter of who was going to win, the Dutch or the Germans.

"We'll win because we're stronger," he said confidently. Janna wondered. Seeing so much of Hugo, Mina, Sef, and Corrie had made her aware of the resistance in the hearts of the Dutch. Could you really win if you did not have the hearts of the people? Could you conquer hearts by force?

Janna had been thinking a lot about Hugo. She felt sorry for him. He had sounded so sad when he said he couldn't lead a normal life. Did that mean he could not marry? In a sudden glow of benevolence, she had rubbed her ring and wished him his heart's desire. Now she was waiting impatiently to hear what good fortune had befallen him.

Her father seemed to be thinking of Hugo too. "He might be foolish enough to try and come here today," he said. "The poor fellow, they might do something to him. I'll go and meet him."

"No, no, don't, something might happen to you," cried Mechtild in a sudden panic. She hung on his arm. "Don't go out."

"Nothing will happen to me," said Otto. "I'm a German, remember?" But Mechtild flung her arms around Otto and would not let him go. Janna watched approvingly.

"Come, Mechtild," Otto said at last, "I'm not going to the end of the world." He disengaged himself and left.

Corrie hadn't come, so Janna was faced with all the work. Meals were simple, just opening cans. Cleaning kerosene lamps was a different matter. She had to run to Mina for advice.

Mechtild helped to get the lunch ready. They were both in the kitchen when Otto returned. He looked white and shaken. There was blood on his hands and his shirt. He fell into a chair.

"Don't get excited now, don't get excited," he warned, waving a hand. This only alarmed the others more.

"You had an accident!" cried his wife. "I knew something would happen! I *knew* it … Why didn't you listen to me?"

"I'm all right," said Otto. "It's not me, it's Hugo, that blasted little idiot, that crazy fool…"

"Otto…what *happened*?"

"You know people are forbidden to gather in the streets during martial law. A necessary measure. They're shot on sight, without warning, if they do. We've been arming the Dutch National Socialists to help keep order. They're just a lot of trigger-happy louts. A few women were standing in front of an announcement of recent executions. Perfectly innocent. They were probably looking for the names of friends or relatives. One had a small boy by the hand. Along comes that armed scum and starts shooting at them. They scream…and who rushes to their rescue? Our little hero, Hugo! He shouts at the Dutchmen not to shoot their own people, or something to that effect, and they laugh at him, call him names in their sweet Dutch way, and start to aim at the little boy to spite him. Hugo moves like lightning and gets the bullet in his own heart."

Janna gave a cry and flung herself into her mother's arms.

"I was still at a distance, but as soon as I got there, I gave those thugs a piece of my mind! I told them I'd inform Herr Rauter of what they had done. That scared them. They were probably already sobered by the harm they had done. Anyway, they went off. The women and the little boy had gone too, leaving Hugo lying there, in his own blood...I lifted him up, he was as light as a child. He smiled at me, moved his lips as if to say something, and he died in my arms. At least he was pronounced dead when I got him to the hospital."

Herr Oster looked at his bloodstained hands. "I liked that little fellow," he said. Janna whimpered in her mother's arms. "It comes from giving guns to ruffians," her father continued. "We Germans have to bear the blame for this. I'm ashamed." There was a silence, broken only by Janna's sobs.

"Well, I suppose it was the way he'd want to die," Otto said heavily after a while. The words pierced Janna's heart. Her wish! Of course! But she hadn't meant anything like that...she wanted Hugo to be happily married. She would have rejected this answer if she had known. What kind of queer magic did the ring have? It made no sense. For Hugo wasn't a "little fellow" as her father kept calling him. Hugo was great. His mind and heart could have been of service to Holland for a long time. He himself might think the life of the little boy worth more than his own, but Janna doubted it. People like Hugo were rare. Janna had never met anyone like him, and now she had to learn to live without him. Never again could she ask him questions...She was a murderer like Cain.

"I don't know where to look for another tutor," she heard her father say. "All young men are being called up for labor, or interned as members of the Dutch Army."

Janna tore herself out of her mother's embrace. "I won't have another tutor, I won't!" she screamed. "Never, never!" She collapsed in a storm of tears. Her mother vainly tried to hush her. Her father stroked her hair.

"There, there, darling," he said. "I wish I could take you away from all this. I wish we'd never taken you out of the Black Forest..." Janna drew back and looked at her father through drenched eyelashes.

"Left me there?" she asked. "I'd have hated that. I'm glad you sent for me."

"I thought you were happy there," said her father.

"I was then," Janna admitted, wiping her eyes on her sleeve. Her father gave her his handkerchief and she blew her nose.

"But I learned so much here; I'd rather know people like Hugo even if they get killed than never know them at all." Her father looked at her in bewilderment. His face was good and honest and loving, but Janna saw clearly, for the first time, that there would always be a barrier between her and her father because there were things he would never understand. Was that why her mother had turned to the Baron? Yet it did not stop Janna from loving her father.

When she told Sef about Hugo's death, she found sensitive understanding. "Poor Janneke," he said, stroking her hair. "To have made such a friend and to lose him so suddenly! But from what you tell me he seems to have had a great spirit in a very frail shell. Perhaps there wasn't much for him to look forward to in this life. There is another life, you know, Janna, and in that life you may meet again."

"Do you really think so?" Janna looked up at him with wet eyes. In Germany most young people did not believe these things any more. Only older ones. Sef nodded. His eyes seemed wiser than his age. Janna thought he looked as if he had suffered much, young as he was.

She gazed around the little room and noticed how dirty it was beginning to look. "I'm going to clean this place," she announced. She didn't want Mina to see it like this when she was up again. Besides, good hard scrubbing might cure her depression and guilt feelings.

"That's not necessary," said Sef. "I'm very comfortable. You look after me splendidly, little Muff."

"I prefer Janneke," said Janna.

Sef grinned. "That's only for special occasions," he said.

"The room has got to be cleaned," Janna decreed firmly.

"Very well, then, but don't disturb the papers on my table." Janna fetched a pail and other necessary articles and brought them to her room. She fastened the hook on her door and entered Sef's room.

"I'm going to the chapel," said Sef, obviously fearing her domestic armory. Janna did a thorough job. She pulled the sheets from the bed, replacing them with clean ones from the linen closet. She swept and scrubbed the floor. In a corner she found a crumpled piece of yellow cloth. She unfolded it. It was a star with the black word "Jew" across the middle. A Jewish star! How had that got here? Had the van Arkels been hiding Jews? That was *really* dangerous. That was the worst they could do, worse than making weapons. If that were found out, they'd be finished, wherever they were. They'd have to share the fate of the Jews...perhaps be sent to a gas chamber...She was staring at the little yellow cloth when Sef came through the trapdoor.

"Oh, I see you've found my star," Sef said cheerfully. "I wondered where it had gone to!"

His star...Sef's star...

And then she knew! Like an electric shock the knowledge ran through her, making her understand a lot of things.

Sef was a Jew.

The Lost Siegfried

Janna felt miserable. She had spoiled everything. She had angered Sef, yet she hadn't been able to help it. She had had an instant revulsion as soon as she had heard from Sef's own lips that he was a Jew. It was a hated, despised word, full of dark associations. Never before had she come face to face with her prejudice, because never before had it touched her personally. But Sef was in her heart now, and it was over her heart as well as over his head that all the evil stories and caricatures she had grown up with had spilled like poison. She felt betrayed, as if Sef had done it on purpose, got her friendship on false pretenses. He said it had never occurred to him that she hadn't guessed.

"Why did you think I was in hiding all the time?"

"Well, you are a Resistance worker, and nearly of age to be sent to Germany…"

"Underground workers have papers and passes and can walk around when they are not under immediate suspicion. If I weren't Jewish, I could prove I wasn't the right age yet." Janna saw that she had been stupid.

"But…but you're fair and…"

"And I haven't got a crooked nose," Sef said. "We don't all look like your caricatures. There are a lot of blond Jews."

"Your name…"

"Sef stands for Josef. That's Jewish enough! Anyway, what did you want me to do? Ring a little bell, like they did in the Middle Ages, to show you're a leper? Or did you want me to wear my star?" He had grown very angry. He went on to say that it was nobody's business what he was. If he wanted to hide that he was Jewish, he had a right to. His ancestry was his own private business, something given him by God. He was himself. If that wasn't enough for people, they could fly to the moon. If Janna felt that way, he was through with her. He'd rather be Jewish than German. Someday Germans would crawl on their bellies trying to hide *their* ancestry.

It had been alarming and Janna had fled in tears. She had to talk to somebody about it and who was there but Mina? But Mina's reaction was almost worse than Sef's. She was like an erupting volcano, spewing out long-suppressed feelings. Her language bristled with Biblical texts.

"So Sef isn't good enough for you, is he?" she spat out with bitter irony. "You have something against him; God's choice does not appeal to you. It's not enough that the poor boy has lost his family and has been cooped up here for years, you must add your little bit to his load! And what are you yourself? Where do you come from? Germans have been laying waste the lands of Europe again and again. What they are now doing to the Jews is unforgivable. We don't know the rights of it yet, but we will know, after we've beaten your country to a pulp. Oh yes, we will. God is on our side, not because we're so good, but because you're so evil. It would be obscene if Hitler won. What we hear from Radio Orange makes our flesh creep...gas chambers, mass graves, corpses piled high...my God, what are you, devils from hell?

"You may be glad if you get a peep into the heaven God has prepared for your victims, for truly you have plowed wickedness, you have reaped iniquity. Only when the wicked man turns away from his wickedness that he hath committed and doeth what is lawful and right shall he save his soul alive. But until then your brother's blood crieth to God from the ground. Go, Janna, I don't want to see you...I was beginning to forget you were German, but sooner or later it shows."

Janna slunk off like a whipped dog, appalled at what Mina had said, smarting under her contempt, and bewildered as to how she had earned it. She finally flung herself on her bed and cried herself to sleep.

Then she had a dream. She was trying to find her way through a thick forest. Branches slapped her face, thorns pricked her, but she had to go on. Something was pursuing her. Then she heard singing: "Today we own Germany, tomorrow the world!" She stood still. Why was she running? Those were her friends, the Hitler Youth. Of course! She could see Hildegarde and Kurt. They marched with blood-red banners flaunting black swastikas. She ran to meet them, but they shouted, "Go away, don't come near us, you are wearing a star!" Something was burning her shoulder. She tore it off. It was a yellow star with a black word on it. She threw it down, but another grew, a bigger one. The Hitler Youth laughed and jeered and whistled. She tore this one off too. Blood was flowing down. It hurt.

"She loves the star! She loves the star!" they chanted. Janna trampled on the star and it cried. It cried like a baby! She picked it up. It *was* a baby, a little baby, crying its heart out.

Now the Hitler Youth behind her became a raging mob.

"You're a traitor!" they shouted. "Give us the baby. Give it up!" Janna knew they would hurt it. She was running again. The baby cried piteously. Its face looked like a monkey's with liquid brown eyes. Her pursuers were very near. Janna's breath was almost gone. The shouting behind her became a howling, a long-drawn-out wolfish howling... Just as she thought she could run no more, she saw a house, a Dutch house with a sawtoothed gable. The door opened and there stood Nella. She took the baby and it stopped crying. She shut the door. Outside, the Hitler Youth howled. Nella's mother came down the stairs.

"They are only wolves," she said. "They don't know any better. Oh! You're *hurt*..." Janna looked at her breast. She saw a deep, star-shaped wound. Shame overwhelmed her. She ran out of the back of the house into her own village in the Black Forest. She went to Erna's house. She ran in.

"I'm home, I'm home," she cried. But Erna turned her back on her. The old mother was staring at something beyond Janna. Her mouth fell open and her rosary beads rattled to the floor. There was beautiful singing behind Janna. She turned around. It was night. The dark sky shone and twinkled with stars, millions and billions of stars, a whole Milky Way of them, and all the stars were singing and slowly descending to the earth. Half floating, half gliding they came, a long, glittering procession. They stood at the bank of a river, their light reflected in long, liquid streamers. Each star was a shining wound on the breast of a white-robed angel, which bloomed and glowed. Very sweet music came from their voices and their hands reached out to Janna.

"Come, you are one of us."

"No, I'm not." Janna said it with sorrow now, with humility. "It's all a mistake, I belong to the wolves…I can't cross the river…" The voices faded, the stars melted into a mist. Behind Janna there was a loud howling. As she turned, she saw ferocious jaws with great teeth and lolling tongues …Mean little eyes gleamed at her, hungrily…There was no escape…She was alone…

With a cry she woke. Her cheeks were wet with tears. She lay on her back thinking. Sef and Mina were angry with her, and it weighed on her. It had been so wonderful, their friendship. Why had Sef's race come to spoil it? Sef had said that God had given him his race. That was true. He must have been hurt by what she had said. She had not been thinking of Sef, had she? She had only been occupied with her own feelings. For the first time she realized the deadly danger Sef was in, had been in for several years. The risk of being an underground worker was bad enough. But an underground worker still had a right to live; he would only be punished for what he did. A Jew was guilty regardless; he was punished just for breathing.

What Sef must have suffered! Was that why he never spoke of his parents? Had his parents been among those faces staring out of the cattle cars? Had those terrible things Mina had mentioned happened to *them*? How could Sef *bear* it! Now she knew why he worked so hard on those forgeries. Janna wept quietly. Mina was right, Janna had been arrogant. Being German was not something to be proud of...

Timidly she knocked at the wardrobe panel. A gentle voice said, "Come in." She saw Sef sitting despondently on his chair, his head bowed.

"Oh Sef," she said. What had she done...added to all his sufferings! "Oh Sef, I've hurt you...I didn't mean to..."

"Poor Janna," said Sef. "I understand. I was brutal to you. I've just been thinking what it must have meant to you to be indoctrinated against Jews all your life and then unknowingly make friends with one. It was hard on you, I admit it."

"No, I was wrong," said Janna. "Can you forgive me? I really like you just as much...it's only...only..."

"You've lost your Siegfried," said Sef, smiling.

"Yes, how did you know?" asked Janna wonderingly. "That's exactly it."

"So I'm just Sef now. That's good. That's what I want to be."

"Oh Sef..." Janna smiled through her tears. She felt happy. It was over. Sef and she were together again. She looked at him. Yes, he was Sef, entirely Sef. Not "a Jew." What was "a Jew"? She had no idea. There were Peters and Hildes and Corries and Sefs. There wasn't "a" anything. She'd made a fuss about nothing.

The Picture

Janna and Mina made up. They both apologized. "I had no right to go for you like that," Mina said penitently. "The Good Book says: 'Thou shalt not seethe a kid in his mother's milk,' and you're only a child, you can't help what you're taught. Say no more about it."

Despite the strike, Mina had a visit from her brother. Janna opened the door for him: a huge figure of a man who looked as if a little political upheaval was beneath his notice. He left his wooden shoes outside and entered on coarsely knit stocking feet. He looked at Janna with Mina's eyes under Mina's eyebrows. He removed a flat cap.

"I had to see what the old one's gone and done now," he boomed. "What's she been up to, eh? Did you go skipping rope with her? Here, lookit, I brought her some of my best blooms." He was carrying lovely, fragrant hyacinths wrapped in a newspaper.

"Well," he said, wiping his face with a red handkerchief, "I see as you've had a bit of trouble here. Lots of police about. They did not bother me none. I'm too big." With a hearty chuckle he mounted the stairs, his corduroy pants squeaking. He stayed a long time with Mina. When Janna brought them up some coffee and crackers he said, "How would you like it if I took that young man away from you? Would you miss him?" Janna looked questioningly at Mina.

"He knows about Sef," said Mina, who was looking younger and pretty in her joy at having her brother there. "He was saying he could use Sef.

He keeps several underdivers...people in hiding, you know. They help him with his bulb farm. I've told him Sef does more important work here, and it's safe here. No one is going to search the home of an SD official."

Janna gazed at her dumbly, appalled at the idea of losing Sef.

"He'd miss you too, I guess," the bulb farmer said with twinkling eyes.

Janna found her tongue. "Oh no, he won't. He likes another girl," she said. "He has her picture pinned up."

"Is that so?" said Mina's brother with a quizzical look on his florid face. "My, my, I wonder where his eyes are!"

"Stop teasing the girl, Meindert," said Mina, for Janna was blushing.

After Mina's brother had left, Janna asked her, "Is he your only relative?"

"He is my twin. My parents are dead. When we were small, people said we could have been identical, we were so alike. Of course, now you see the difference." She smiled. "Meindert and Mina, we were a pair, I can tell you!" She looked dreamily back into the past. Then she shook herself. "We must do something about that picture. It has to be hidden where your mother did not look before. The only place I can think of is that old stove in the kitchen, the one we don't use any more."

"And if it doesn't fit?"

"Oh, it will. The lid is large. It used to be a wood stove, burning logs."

"But won't they suspect you of hiding it?" Janna asked anxiously.

"Suspect the cook," asked Mina, eyebrows high, "and risk missing my pastries? Never! Anyway, I've plenty of time to think up an answer if they do. 'In vain is the net spread in sight of the bird.' When will you hide the picture?"

"In the night, that's safest," said Janna.

It was a quiet night, without flak or bombings. People slept deeply. When Janna was sure her parents had gone to bed and she had listened to her father's snores, she put the hook on her door and knocked at the wardrobe panel. Sef was ready for her. He had lit a candle. His face looked weirdly handsome in its glow. Together they crept down the ladder and

THE PICTURE

Sef started the mechanism that made the altar rotate into view. There was the picture, to Janna's relief. She'd had a moment's panic that it might have disappeared. Sef lifted it down and Janna took it in her arms. It was heavy.

"There goes the van Arkel treasure," said Sef. The flickering light set shadows dancing about them.

"You stay here," said Janna. "I'll hide the picture."

"No, I'm coming with you," said Sef. "There's no danger, everyone is asleep." They padded softly through the long room, Sef carrying the picture. As they went down the staircase to the kitchen the stairs creaked. They stopped and listened, but all was still.

Janna lifted the lid of the old stove. It looked very dirty inside and gave out a musty smell.

"You must wrap the picture," whispered Sef. They went looking for paper and string. Janna thought she saw some on top of a cupboard. As she pulled it down, a photograph came with it. It dropped on the floor. Sef gave a cry and picked it up.

"Sh!" warned Janna. "They'll hear you!"

"My photograph ..." whispered Sef. "My precious, missing picture. How did it get up there? Mina must have stuck it there and forgotten about it. My *picture!*" Janna looked over his shoulder. He had sunk down on a kitchen chair, and in his emotion he had let the candle lean over so that wax was dripping on the floor. Janna took it from him and held it near to light the picture. It was a happy group portrait of a family: a thoughtful father with high forehead and deep, searching eyes; a gentle, blond mother, and two children: one a laughing minx of about four with dancing ringlets, the other obviously Sef, when he was about Janna's age.

"Is that your family?" whispered Janna. Sef nodded. A tear was trickling down his cheek. "It's all I have left of them," he whispered. "I'm so glad I found it."

"What happened to them?" asked Janna.

"Do you have to ask?" Sef's voice was unsteady. His hands had clenched into fists. "They were taken soon after the invasion. My father was a well-known artist, and he had been quite outspoken. He would not tell lies or prevaricate, not even to save our lives. What had to be had to be, he said. He wasn't going to skulk like a criminal when he had done nothing wrong. I only escaped because I was staying with the van Arkels. It was Willem van Arkel's birthday. They kept me with them and treated me like a son."

"And what happened to your parents?"

"I never heard from them. Some people who returned from the concentration camp at Vught said they had been seen there but were sent on to Poland. We know what that means…" Sef's cheeks had turned waxen and his forehead was moist as he gave a low groan. "I lie awake thinking of them sometimes…" he muttered. "What it was like…and my poor little sister…" Janna wanted to comfort him but did not dare. It was her people who had done this to him. At last she asked, "Couldn't the Dutch people have protected them?"

"The van Arkels would have sheltered them, but it happened too quickly, long before the regular raids. Anyway, I doubt whether my parents would have accepted their help. The real trouble was that no one really believed such terrible things could happen. I suppose we were too civilized." Sef sighed. "Later we realized that before we surrendered to the Muffs we should have burned all our records, and when stars were prescribed, everyone should have worn them. We should never have let any part of our Dutch people be singled out." Sef was silent. The candle flame sputtered a bit. A moth was trying to warm its wings on it.

"People confuse law with virtue," Sef went on. "The Dutch especially. They think it wrong to oppose a law, even if it is an evil one. Of course it was a strain. We were hoping to be liberated before much harm was done, but now I wonder if any of us Jews will survive."

"Yes, those you're saving with your fake papers," Janna said encouragingly.

Sef shrugged. "So few," he murmured.

Janna began to wrap the Rembrandt in the coarse brown paper she had found. She tied it with some string out of the table drawer. Sef tucked his precious photograph inside his jacket. He helped Janna knot the string tightly. They hid the painting in the old stove. Then, with their stump of candle, they climbed upstairs to their beds.

The next day the strike was over and the house returned to normal, though in the rest of Holland martial law continued and people were executed, even children of thirteen. On the fifth day of May the occupation authorities proclaimed that all students who had refused to sign the loyalty declaration would have to labor in Germany, otherwise their parents would be held responsible.

Janna mourned Hugo. She bitterly missed her lessons.

She and Mina had decided to let Heinz find the picture. They felt sorry for the boy, who was scolded by grownups all day long and beaten by his father at night. Janna could not listen to his screams any more, now that she knew what caused them. She had to put her fingers in her ears and go under the bedclothes. She told Sef about it. He had heard the screams too.

"We in Holland always said the Germans were too strict," he commented. "We think that such harsh, inhuman treatment fitted your people for a dictatorship."

"My parents treat me kindly," Janna said.

"Ah, but you're a girl," Sef answered.

After breakfast, on the morning following the hiding of the picture, Janna did not shoo Heinz out of the kitchen when he wanted to help. She let him dry the dishes. Then she looked at the old stove and said, "I wonder why they keep that useless thing here. It's only taking up room." Heinz needed no further encouragement. He ran to it and looked inside.

"There's something hidden here," he shouted. "Look!" Triumphantly he pulled out the parcel and unwrapped it, tearing at the paper and tugging at the string till Janna cut it with a carving knife. She made suitable noises of astonishment as she wiped her sudsy hands and found a safe place for the picture, leaning against the top half of a dresser. Heinz had guessed immediately that it was the Rembrandt—he'd probably heard his parents talking about it—and he was so proud and exultant that he ran through the house, banging doors and shouting the good news. Soon everyone was gathered in the kitchen: Herr and Frau Frosch, Herr and Frau Oster (whose rehearsals were starting again that day), and Corrie. Everyone gaped at the painting. Heinz earned his full measure of praise, even from his father, who went so far as to say he was proud of his son. Heinz glowed.

Herr Frosch telephoned Herr Rauter, who came over right away. He was a stocky man with a coarse complexion and a scarred face. He wore the uniform of Höhere SS und Polizeiführer. His thin lips closed, he looked around with gimlet eyes.

"You're lucky you found the picture," he said to Janna's father, looking sideways at him. There was a note of irony in his voice. "We had just got notice to arrest you." Herr Oster was too angry to answer this. He kept still. People did not talk back to the head of police. Herr Rauter was examining the stove that had hidden the picture.

He sniffed suspiciously. "Curious place," he muttered. "Did the cook put it there?"

Herr Frosch took a step forward. His voice trembled as he said, "I vouch for the cook, a loyal soul, above suspicion..."

Herr Rauter laughed. "You'd be surprised," he said. "When my men get at her...Where is she? Why doesn't she vouch for herself?"

"Because she sustained an injury in her devoted service to this family, Herr Polizeiführer," gabbled Herr Frosch.

Herr Rauter gave a disagreeable snicker. "You're afraid for your omelets," he sneered. Then, with a shrug of the shoulders, he abandoned a possible victim. "Very well, the picture is here. We'll spare your cook if you'll lend her to me sometimes when I have a party."

"Oh yes, certainly, Herr Rauter," Herr Frosch said, bowing obsequiously. Janna wondered what Mina would think of that.

Herr Oster cleared his throat. "I want my wife and me relieved of all further responsibility for this picture," he said. "We have been unjustly accused of stealing it."

"There is no proof that you didn't," Herr Rauter answered sharply. "Only that you changed your mind... just in time." He gave a sardonic look at the stove.

For a moment Herr Oster was silenced. Then he broke out angrily, "You'd better remove the thing to your office. I see we are still under suspicion."

"Tut, tut," said Herr Rauter, waving his hand. "I did not go as far as that. I merely pointed out that there was no proof."

"It is better for you to take it," Herr Oster insisted. "We have no safe here."

"Impossible," said Herr Rauter. "There are procedures that have to be followed. We have to arrange for proper transportation under armed guard."

"In that case, give it to Herr Frosch. I want nothing further to do with it," Herr Oster insisted.

"Yes, yes," Herr Frosch interrupted eagerly. "I will take good care of it. I will put it in my sitting room and have a second lock made on the door and put a watch in front; no burglar will be able to get at it." He was rubbing his hands with pleasure at the honor of guarding a possession of the Führer's.

"Give it to me in writing," said Herr Oster. "I'm not to be held responsible any more." His voice shook with anger. Herr Rauter looked impatient but sat down at the kitchen table and wrote a few lines on a scrap of paper to the effect that the picture had been removed from the Osters' custody. He signed it with a flourish and gave it to Otto, who pocketed it carefully. Herr Frosch picked up the Rembrandt and bore it reverently upstairs.

Janna ran to tell Mina what had happened, and as soon as it was safe, she visited Sef.

"There won't be any living with Heinz now, he is so proud at having been the one to find the picture," Janna told him, smiling. "It's even better than spying on the neighbors!"

"I'm sorry for him," said Sef. "I'm sorry for all the young people in Germany. What a way to grow up! And they'll bear the brunt of the reaction later, when we've won the war. They'll have to build up the new Germany. Mynheer van Arkel always said that Hitler's greatest crime was what he did to his own people, the way he used the idealism and enthusiasm of youngsters for his own nefarious purposes." Janna nodded, thinking of Kurt. Where was he now, in a training camp?

"Tell me about the van Arkels," she said. "Tell me about Willem. Was he the oldest boy?"

Sef nodded. "He was my best friend. I was in the same class with him at school until the Germans came and threw me out. I had to attend a Jewish school then. Do you know I never realized that being Jewish made me different until the Germans came? My parents were tolerant and liberal. We had our own services, but so had the Protestants and Catholics. My father always said there was but one God and everyone worshipped Him in their own way. What mattered was to be honest and upright and kind. At school we were all equals. Willem and I used to go on Boy Scout trips or we went hunting plover eggs in the fields on a March morning. Plover eggs are a great delicacy—you could get money for them—and we always needed money for our projects. We built huts and made hutches for rabbits…When the invasion came and Holland fell, Willem and Maurits, his younger brother, and I built a boat. It was the queerest tub you ever saw, made out of Heineken's beer barrels. It had a sail and was seaworthy. We managed to reach the open sea in it. We intended to sail to England but we got a head wind which stranded us on one of the northern islands. The coast guard caught us and might have shot us if our boat hadn't looked so wacky. They believed us when we said we'd been accidentally swept out to sea. The hardest thing was to seem grateful for being rescued!" Janna had listened, full of admiration. But she heard Heinz shouting for her, so she could not stay.

Herr Frosch gloried in his custody of the picture. He made a great fuss putting in the extra lock and displayed the key on every possible occasion. Heinz wanted to stand guard over it, he felt a proprietary right in the picture, but his father installed a policeman. Janna had to pass him every time she brought Mina her food. She noticed she was beginning to fear the Gestapo as much as the Dutch did.

During the following days, many friends and acquaintances of Herr Frosch were invited to admire the Rembrandt. Janna met so many strangers on the stairs she took the way through the long room to visit Sef. She was going to him one morning when she heard voices in the anteroom. Herr Frosch's and another somewhat familiar voice…Where had she heard it? She slipped quickly behind the draperies in the long room, vaguely alarmed.

There they were, coming through the glass doors, Herr Frosch and… yes! The fat man from the train. Like an enormous ghost from the past, he waddled behind Herr Frosch, who was talking rapidly.

"Great honor, great responsibility," he was saying. "I told Herr Polizeiführer that we'd better have some professional advice about packing the picture. Can't take the chance of having it damaged, you understand. It's going to Berchtesgaden. Herr Rauter said you might cast your eyes over the other pictures. Perhaps there is something else Hitler might fancy."

"Certainly, certainly," the fat man said unctuously. He had his cameras slung over his shoulders and carried a tripod. "Why not have some pictures taken?" His small eyes gleamed.

"Yes, yes, that might be a good idea," Herr Frosch said nervously. "But not today." The fat man was starting to put up his tripod. "I'd have to consult Herr Rauter, you understand, and we'd have to know about prices."

"Oh, our gallery is very reasonable," the fat man assured him.

"Yes, Herr Stolz, but I'm not the one to decide that," said Herr Frosch. "You'll be able to send a man to pack the Rembrandt then?"

"When is the picture going?" asked the fat man, who was peering at the pictures on the walls. "Or hasn't that been decided yet?"

"Oh yes, it's been decided," said Herr Frosch. "These things have to be arranged in advance, you know. Friday at ten the van is coming, under armed guard, of course."

"Very well, our man will be here on Thursday," promised the fat man.

"Do you see anything here that would interest the Führer?" asked Herr Frosch.

"Very good pictures," said the fat man, smacking his lips. "There's money here all right, genuine Dutch Impressionists. But not for Hitler, no. He considers Impressionism degenerate. You know perhaps that he is an artist himself? No? I thought that was general knowledge... If he had been accepted at the Viennese Academy, who knows? We might not have a new order in Germany now. On such trifles hangs the world. Now, Göring is another kettle of fish. A real connoisseur of art. Bought a Vermeer here, you know, from a collector called Vermeegheren. An astonishing piece of work... and no one knew it existed. A real find. Hitler was angry not to have been told of such an important picture. Vermeers are very rare, you know. Adolf and Hermann have—what shall I say—a friendly rivalry. They try to snatch pictures away in front of each other's nose and they smash crockery in anger when they do not succeed. The little ways of the mighty! But Göring pays well and Hitler does not.

You would not consider giving the Rembrandt to Göring? It would be much more profitable, I assure you."

"It has nothing to do with me," said Herr Frosch stiffly. "I am merely the custodian. I do what I'm told."

"Ah yes, the loyal servant," said Herr Stolz with profound admiration. "What would our Reich do without them! Never thinking of gain, dutifully anchored to their desks, signing documents that bring life or death to others. Admirable. Ah, look at that. A genuine Israels! Göring would covet that."

"It's painted by a Jew," said Herr Frosch contemptuously. "He wouldn't want that."

"You don't mean it." Herr Stolz sounded astonished.

"It's a Jewish name," Herr Frosch pointed out.

"Yes, but I'm surprised you'd reject the picture, which is worth a lot of money, for that reason. I did not think that there was anything valuable the Jews possessed that you could not use. Live and learn, I say."

"I don't know what you mean," Herr Frosch said stiffly.

"Ah, I see. If you only rob on a sufficiently large scale, it becomes invisible. You're sure you don't want a photograph?" He sighed. "A pity, the light is excellent today."

"Shall I show you the Rembrandt now?" asked Herr Frosch, who had been unable to follow the twists and turns of the fat man's conversation. He preceded Herr Stolz into the anteroom. "If your man will come Thursday night with the necessary material, I'll make sure…" His voice faded.

Janna emerged from her hiding place. She had a cramp in her leg and rubbed it. She wondered what the fat man was up to. He had been much too polite. She went to tell Sef about it. As she recounted the story of her train journey, she found at last a perfect listener.

"You backed the wrong horse there," Sef told her, smiling. "The fat man was right, the little one was obviously a Jew. I hope he got away, poor fellow."

"Oh!" said Janna. How stupid she had been! It all came from having such a distorted idea of Jews, she hadn't been able to recognize one when she saw him. She had half believed the story that they had cloven hoofs.

"I don't like your fat man," Sef went on. "I'll keep the door of the chapel locked from now on. He is quite capable of stealing the big picture and exposing this place."

That was true; Janna hadn't thought of that.

"He was more interested in the Israels, though," she said.

On Thursday the man from the art dealer came to pack the painting. Herr Frosch was taking no chances. He supervised the work and never let the picture out of his sight. On Friday the van arrived under armed Gestapo guards, looking formidable. Herr Frosch put his valuable parcel in their keeping and signed a paper they gave him.

"Aren't you supposed to give me a receipt?" he asked.

"That won't be necessary," they said. "Goodbye, Herr Frosch." The van roared off.

A day later, at breakfast, there was a telephone call for Herr Frosch. The phone was just outside the dining room. They all heard Herr Frosch's anguished cries.

"No, no! Impossible! I signed for it ... They were armed guards of the SD. What do you mean, gagged and bound? They were SD men, I saw their insignia ... Switched uniforms? How is it possible? What do you mean, you don't believe me? Of course I signed, they told me to ... Everything was in order. A declaration that the picture was to go to Göring? No, no, I did not sign that. It was a release ... well, they said it was. I did not read the whole thing, there was no time. It was all correct, in order, I tell you ... Well, why not get the picture back from Göring? Surely the Führer can command what he wants? Well, ask Herr Stolz from the art gallery. He said something about Göring and I told him

I was not authorized. You heard he's gone? Herr Stolz has vanished? My God, I should have known he was a scoundrel! Herr Rauter…Herr Rauter… He's hung up!"

The family at the breakfast table had listened spellbound. Herr Frosch staggered to his seat, looking ten years older. Frau Oster quickly poured him more coffee.

"What's wrong?" she asked.

"The picture!" he groaned, placing his elbows on the table and holding his head. "There's been foul play! The real guards were found bound and gagged in a shed and the people I handed the picture to were agents of Göring. It has been sent to Göring, not Hitler, and Hitler is furious."

"It's not possible!" exclaimed Frau Oster. Frau Frosch was trembling. She spilled her coffee. She's afraid Herr Frosch will take it out on her, thought Janna. Heinz stared fixedly at his father, forgetting to eat.

"The trouble is, Herr Rauter won't believe I had nothing to do with it," Herr Frosch continued, gulping his food. "Herr Stolz has disappeared. Of course he did it."

"Why doesn't Hitler tell Göring to give back the picture?" asked Frau Frosch.

"He'd have to buy it back," explained her husband. "Hitler would have got it for nothing, but Göring paid a considerable sum. Besides, he can't afford to offend Göring, who is very popular and the head of the air force. Hitler took a lot of trouble to get that picture and now it's all coming to nothing. Of course he is angry."

"What will he do to you, Father?" asked Heinz.

"Nothing, son. To me he can do nothing. I'm innocent," his father answered. But his optimism was misplaced. Someone had to suffer for Hitler's displeasure and Herr Rauter was determined that it should not be himself. Having signed that paper, Herr Frosch was the obvious scapegoat. The Osters were out of it, thanks to Herr Rauter's scribble.

The fact that Herr Frosch had acted in perfect good faith did not matter. As he himself had often asserted, his government was ruthless. He was clapped into prison.

Heinz was furious. Janna caught him tearing the pictures from the walls of his room and rending the flag into shreds. He stamped and spat on them.

"I'll never be a Hitler Youth," he shouted. "I hate Hitler. My father is innocent!"

Janna marveled. Heinz was destroying what he had admired and believed in for the sake of a father who had beaten him almost every night. But she liked him better than she ever had.

Frau Frosch, after weeping in her room for several days, cheered up when she got a letter from her parents inviting her and Heinz to make their home with them. Frau Frosch explained to the Osters that her parents had a farm not far from Hamburg. "Heinz will be able to go to school and make friends," she exulted. The next week Frau Frosch and Heinz left, on a beautiful May morning, while the birds were twittering and the canals reflected the blue sky. Heinz and Janna shook hands solemnly. Heinz had grown up. He was no longer the little monkey who had stuck his tongue out at Janna. Janna was different too. Now she had respect for Heinz. Beside him, his mother looked like a schoolgirl going home.

When Janna and Corrie were cleaning out the Frosches' apartment, Janna found a crumpled letter stuck in a drawer. It was signed "Erich Stolz." She could not resist reading it.

Honored Sir,
I'm writing this just before boarding a plane—to South America—which Göring has obligingly lent me. I want to apologize for any inconvenience I may have caused you, and to thank you for your cooperation in supplying the details concerning the removal of the

picture. I also want to point out to you that I was willing to go halves with you. We could have cleaned up the Impressionists at the same time. However, I did not wish to sully what you obviously regarded as your honor; I am glad I am not hampered that way. Meanwhile, I forgive you for any unkind thoughts you may have had about me. I have obtained enough money to enable me to forgive my worst enemies. Hoping that you'll be able to talk yourself out of an awkward situation. I remain

Yours sincerely,
Erich Stolz

(My future address, for obvious reasons, will remain a secret, so you need not answer this.)

Janna laughed aloud. She realized with surprise that you could like and dislike someone at the same time.

The Ball

GERMANY WAS LOSING HEAVILY ON ALL FRONTS. In the kitchen Mina and Corrie rejoiced. Mina was on her feet again, though she still had to take it easy. She was full of Biblical predictions.

"Who sheddeth man's blood, by man shall his blood be shed" and "They have no rest day or night who worship the Beast and his image. But they that wait upon the Lord shall renew their strength: they shall mount up with wings as eagles, they shall run and not be weary, they shall walk and not faint."

Sef also gloried in the Allied victories. Janna was happy for them, but sobered by the thought that it was her own country that was losing and might be laid waste. She had seen the destruction of Cologne while Hitler's armies were still advancing. What would happen when vengeful soldiers trampled the fertile valleys and entered the little villages, she shuddered to think.

She could not wish for Germany's victory. She knew by now that even the Baron did not wish for that. But she hoped that Germany might rise again and become happy and prosperous with a new, merciful government.

There was a general feeling that the Allied invasion was not far off. The German Army was gathering around the coastline, studying maps, guessing what the enemy was going to do.

Visitors coming to the house seemed nervous and reckless. Janna wondered about the Baron. What was he thinking now? The house was dull without Heinz's shrill voice and his pranks.

But the worst was her mother's depression. Mechtild seemed to have lost interest in everything. She drifted vaguely through the days, rather like Frau Frosch. Otto said her acting wasn't up to standard.

"What's the matter?" he asked her one evening after dinner. "Worried about the war? Never fear, Hitler will make a comeback. The man is a genius."

"A genius," said Mechtild listlessly. "Fine genius! Look where he landed us. Dietrich says all he had was beginner's luck."

"Dietrich? Have you seen him?"

"You know I haven't."

Otto looked lovingly at her. He put a hand on her shoulder. "Poor Mechtild, lost her playmate," he said. "You need a diversion. Let's give a party... a ball. The long room is perfect for it!"

Janna's mother cheered up at once. "A fancy-dress ball!" she cried. "A marvelous idea!" She started to make arrangements right away. Janna had to help address invitations. It would be held on a Monday, the actors' night off.

"Are we going to send an invitation to the Baron?" asked Janna. Her mother looked startled and blushed.

"Why not?" she said, brightening. "It would be wrong to leave him out after all he's done for us." Then she said despondently, "Of course he won't come."

Janna could not bear to see her so sad. She surreptitiously rubbed her ring. Let the Baron come to the ball, she wished. After all, what harm could it do, just for one evening, to make her mother happy?

The Baron received his invitation, for he sent cases of champagne, baskets of game, truffles, and pastries. It made her mother weep again.

Mechtild took a lot of trouble repairing her costume, an old-fashioned wedding dress she had found in the attic, dating from the Napoleonic era. Some of the silver beads had fallen off and there were tears in the satin and lace. Janna wanted to be dressed as Brunhilde, so her mother borrowed a costume from the stage wardrobe: flowing white robe, silver breastplates, sandals, shield, helmet, and spear—just as Janna had visualized it for Hildegarde's play. It would be a warm costume to wear in June, but when she saw herself in the mirror, she knew she wouldn't mind the heat.

The costume had to be taken in only a little. "You aren't the little tyke who came here in February," Mechtild said approvingly. "What a difference! You look almost like a young lady."

The evening of the party was warm and sultry. In the long room Janna excitedly slid up and down the golden parquet floor, shining with wax. She'd never been to a ball before. If only Sef could have been with her—but he'd be looking through the peephole in the picture. It made her feel less alone.

It was still light when people began to arrive. Corrie, wearing a new black dress with frilly cap and apron, was kept busy opening the door and taking guests' wraps. She wasn't going to stay late; her father was going to fetch her and take her home after supper had been served.

As people came in, Janna saw one lovely costume after another: a comical Red Riding Hood with a ferocious wolf, a Satan in scarlet with a cow's tail and horns, a Neptune with a three-pronged fork. There were also a lot of Wotans and Freyas and Siegfrieds. The room was filled with chatter and the clinking of glasses. As dusk fell, drapes were pulled across the open windows and the chandeliers were lit. The air became more oppressive and the ladies twirled their fans. Janna had put her shield and spear on a window seat while she handed around appetizers and crackers.

She saw Herr Schmidt and Herr Wolff. They were dressed as wizards, and their beards kept parting from their chins. Otto, who had refused to dress up—he said it was no fun for an actor—stood behind the serving table and poured drinks. Mechtild, in her bridal dress, a wreath of white roses on her head over a diaphanous veil, was, as usual, surrounded by admirers. She had never looked lovelier, thought Janna.

People were beginning to dance to the music of a small band around the piano. Janna watched them, enchanted by the colors, the music, the whirl of movement. A shepherdess lost her crook, a clumsy Tarzan trod on a queen's train; little incidents happened all the time to amuse her. Then her father asked her to dance and she became part of the scene.

"You dance very well," he said. "Where did you learn it?"

"At our Youth meetings," said Janna. "But the boys were always so clumsy. I prefer to dance with you." After a while the atmosphere became stifling and her father put out the lights so he could open the blackout drapes. The orchestra managed with small, shaded lamps behind a screen. Now they were dancing by the moonlight, which was pouring through the open windows along with a smell of honeysuckle and jasmine.

Then Corrie announced, "Supper is served." Janna's father closed the drapes again and the lights went on. People exclaimed over the delicacies on the buffet table in the anteroom. They shoved and jostled to get to it. A beautiful Chinese vase was smashed to bits. They ate carelessly, dropping food on the Turkish carpet, marking polished tables with their glasses, spilling sauce…

"It sounds like thunder," someone said, "and I left my windows open at home."

Janna thought of Sef. She went to the kitchen, but before she had reached the stairs there was a ring at the door. She opened it and there was the Baron, in his ordinary uniform. He didn't seem to see her, didn't answer her greeting. There was a wild look on his face as he gazed beyond her. When Janna turned, she saw her mother, whom some instinct had sent into the hall. Janna stepped back, helpless, and watched what happened with a sinking heart.

"Dietrich…" her mother's voice sang.

"Mechtild…darling…I couldn't stay away…" They were in each other's arms, and there was nothing Janna could do about it. They went downstairs. Janna saw them go into the garden, the romantic garden, where water tinkled in the marble fountain, flowing over the arms and heads of the Rhine maidens; where the moon silvered everything and flowers scented the air... And it was all her own fault.

Unhappily she went into the kitchen and found Mina sitting in a rocking chair, reading the Bible. She started when Janna entered.

"Have you some food for Sef?" Janna asked. "I want to bring it to him. He's missing everything."

"I saved some for him. It's on that plate," said Mina dourly. She started to read out in a sepulchral voice: "'And there was a great earthquake: and the sun became black as sackcloth of hair and the moon became blood and the stars of heaven fell into the earth even as a fig tree casteth her untimely figs, when she is shaken of a mighty wind. And the heaven departed as a scroll when it is rolled together; and every fountain and island were moved out of their places. And the kings of the earth, and the great men, and the rich men, and the chief captains and the mighty men and every bondsman and freed man hid themselves in the dens and in the rocks of the mountains: and said to the mountains and rocks: fall on us and hide us from the face of him that sitteth on the throne, and from the wrath of the Lamb; for the great day of His wrath is come and who shall be able to stand?'"

Janna listened with dismay. "What's that?" she said. She hadn't got further than Moses in her Bible reading.

"It's the vision of St. John," said Mina gloomily. "And I think it's going to happen soon. I feel it in my bones. All this godless cavorting about when people are starving or dying in agony... God will spit out his creatures like saliva."

"You're feeling like that because it's going to storm," said Janna. "Even animals feel queer then."

"I'm not an animal," said Mina. "I know something bad is going to happen. Mark my words, don't say I didn't warn you!"

Janna ran upstairs with the tray, passing some amorous couples on the stairs. Ladies were giggling and fixing their hair in the bathroom.

"Look at Brunhilde. She's got herself a private little feast," they mocked.

"Isn't it nice to be young and not have to mind your manners!"

Janna put the hook on her door and turned the key as well. She crawled through the wardrobe and found Sef at work.

"I thought you were watching," she said.

"I was, until the lights went out," said Sef. He sounded as depressed as Mina.

"Look what I have for you," said Janna. "That's real champagne, and there's a partridge leg, and those pastries are scrumptious."

Sef cheered up. "I'm glad you came," he said. "It's so stuffy in here and I was wondering whether the time would ever come when I could go to parties and dances."

"How old are you?" asked Janna.

"Nearly seventeen," said Sef. "I wish I'd been old enough to be in the army. I wish I'd died fighting the invasion…"

"Oh, please, Sef, you're as bad as Mina," said Janna.

"How bad is Mina?" asked Sef, his eyes twinkling. He finished the fowl and bit into one of the pastries. His face cleared. "They're great," he said. "The Baron's, I suppose. I wonder whose supplies he looted… Thanks for bringing them, little Muff."

"Mina was reading awful bits out of the Bible," said Janna, answering his question. "About the sun falling and the moon bleeding and people covering themselves with rocks."

Sef laughed. "You've really cheered me up, Janna," he said. "I think what was bothering me was that I'd never had a chance to dance, being in hiding all the time. I'll probably die without having learned it."

"I'll teach you now," said Janna.

"Where?"

"In the chapel. You can hear the orchestra there and no one will hear us in all the noise."

"What a good idea!" said Sef. "You're a real friend, Janna." (But not such a friend as Nella, thought Janna with a glance at the photo on the wall.)

As soon as the orchestra started again, Janna and Sef were ready. The music came through clearly. Moonbeams strayed through the ivy and threw weird patterns on the floor. Sef had a good sense of rhythm, and after a few awkward moments they accommodated their movements to each other. When the band struck up a waltz, he seemed to catch on right away. As they whirled around, Janna felt so happy she wished it could go on forever. She marveled at how different it felt to dance with Sef when her father really was the better dancer. This was much more exciting...

"How old are you?" asked Sef in her ear.

"Twelve," she said. "Thirteen next April."

"A baby," sighed Sef. Janna wanted to protest, but she didn't want to interrupt the dancing. She wanted to go on turning and whirling and gliding in Sef's arms forever and ever. We must do this again, she thought. We must do it often... but how to get the music? How could they keep it secret? Oh, she'd find a way...

It was Sef who broke the magic. "You'd better go back," he said. "They might get suspicious if you stay away too long. Remember, we don't have the protection of the SD any more, now that the Frosches are gone." That was true. Janna had not thought of that. She clung to Sef, unwilling to go. He pushed her away, but gently and reluctantly.

"I'll watch you through the peephole," he promised.

"No, no," warned Janna. "A lot of people have been drinking steadily. It isn't safe. Keep the door locked. Promise." She remembered Mina's dire predictions.

"Promise..." she repeated anxiously.

"All right, all right," Sef said, laughing. "You're as moody as a weathercock. I'll go back to work. I feel a lot better than before you came in."

They looked at each other, and in the dim light Sef's eyes seemed like a sea, a greenish sea into which she was slipping, deeper and deeper...till the waves washed over her head...

Sef abruptly turned away his face. "You're quite a girl," he said. "Off you go now."

"All right," Janna said meekly.

She stopped by her balcony and stepped out on it. It was good to breathe the cool, fragrant air. The moon was still shining, but big clouds were massing in opposite directions, proceeding like armies in battle formation. It was completely still. Only the fountain tinkled gently, glittering in the moonlight. And then Janna heard whispers and soft laughter, followed by the deep tones of a man's voice. Her mother and the Baron! They had been out there all through the ages and ages she'd been dancing with Sef! They were in the summerhouse, now a bower of flowering honeysuckle and wild roses. She could see her mother's white dress glimmering between the tendrils. Janna stood rigid, full of dark forebodings. Mina was right, something terrible was going to happen. The Baron would take her mother away, far away, to his castle in Bavaria. They would probably offer to take her too, but she couldn't go. She couldn't leave her father alone; it wouldn't be fair. But to live without her mother! They had become so close lately, ever since Janna knew they shared the horror at what Germany was doing. They had that in common with the Baron as well. Her father would not see it. He was too loyal. To him it was unthinkable that Germany could do wrong.

The clouds had been moving nearer and nearer. Now they enveloped and conquered the moon. Lightning split the sky and for an instant Janna saw her mother and the Baron sitting close together, their arms entwined. Then thunder threw its boulders heavily across the sky and gusts of wind began to shake the trees. Her mother squealed. Another whiplash of lightning showed her getting up, the Baron helping her. Then the rain pelted down, drenching them. Mechtild and the Baron ran. The slanting spears of water pursued them, lashed them like furies.

Janna hurried inside and closed her windows. Leaving the room, she locked it on the outside, pocketing her key. There were too many strangers about. She passed couples on the stairs, smoking cigarettes and scattering ashes. As she got to the second floor, she saw her mother and the Baron coming up from the first. Her mother's breath came fast. Her wreath hung crooked and her veil sagged, but she looked like a queen. Raindrops were scattered over her like pearls. The Baron had a triumphant air.

She hoped this was going to happen. She dressed like a bride on purpose, thought Janna bitterly.

Her mother floated into the ballroom to the strain of a languorous waltz. The Baron followed her, Janna at his heels. She looked for her father. He was telling a funny story in a corner of the room, surrounded by admiring women. When he looked up and saw his wife with the Baron, telltale rain on their heads and shoulders, he stopped in the middle of a sentence, rose and strode toward them, his face glowering. Janna had never seen him look so ugly, except when he was playing Hunding. The play came forcibly to her mind. Something about his red face also suggested that he had been drinking too freely of the Baron's champagne.

"Where have you been?" he shouted at his wife. "Is that a way for a hostess to behave?" He grabbed her roughly by the arm and shook her.

"Let go, you're hurting me," cried Mechtild, all the glow washed from her face.

"I won't let you go," growled her husband. "You're mine, do you hear? Mine!" Janna remembered with horror that those were the very words her father had said in the play. He was shaking Mechtild so roughly that her wreath fell off, scattering petals all over the floor. People had stopped dancing and were gathering to look at this new entertainment. They thought it was a comedy to amuse the guests and clapped. The Baron had been watching, his eyes flashing. As the wreath fell, he could contain himself no longer.

"Let go, Otto," he said ominously. "Let go." This seemed to enrage

Otto more. He grabbed Mechtild by the neck as if to strangle her. The Baron's fist flashed out and hit Otto on the chin. Otto loosened his hold on Mechtild and fell backward. There was a cry from the guests, who began to understand that this was a real fight. The orchestra stopped playing. Mechtild sank to the floor with a moan. Several of her admirers darted forward and picked her up. She was borne off to a quiet corner where she sat down, sobbing.

Otto scrambled up, his face contorted. He sprang at the Baron like a tiger, but the Baron hit him again. Now Otto began to roar as he punched the Baron in the nose. Blood spouted out. Janna covered her eyes with her hands. It was terrible to see them behaving like wild beasts. And the ring was no use to her. If she let her father win, her mother might feel so sorry for the Baron that she would go off with him anyway, and if she let the Baron win, her mother might think he was the better man. Meanwhile, the fight was going on, punctuated by flashes of lightning, which penetrated even the blackout curtains, and deep growling thunder. Suddenly the electric lights went out and the men struggled in the darkness at the end of the room. Janna could hear pants and groans, and the sound of the piano when they fell against it. Then there was a terrific rattle of thunder and simultaneously a blinding flash of lightning, which showed everyone what was happening. The struggling men staggered against the van Arkel picture. Its cord broke. The painting dropped, wobbled, and fell flat on the floor. The lights went on again as suddenly as they had gone out, showing two panting, bedraggled, blood-smeared men gazing stupidly at the wall space the picture had covered. The secret door stood revealed to all.

Twilight of the Gods

Janna did not await further developments. Sef had to be warned at once. She pushed through the crowd of guests, who were exclaiming and commenting on the surprising discovery, and sped up the stairs to her room. She met Mina in the hall and whispered to her what had happened. Mina needed no long explanations. With trembling fingers Janna unlocked her door. She shut it and fastened the hook. They both rushed into Sef's room.

"You must fly," cried Mina. "They've discovered the door!"

"It's locked," said Sef.

"Good, that'll give us some time. Help me, Janna, we'll pull up the ladder." Janna and Mina opened the trapdoor and pulled up the ladder. It would be some time before Sef's hideout could be reached now. Sef meanwhile was gathering his most needed possessions and putting on the cloak Nella had given him.

"I'll go to Nella," he said.

"No you won't," said Mina, who was gathering up Sef's papers and documents and stuffing them into the fireplace. "You're coming with me, to my brother. I've a bike in the cellar and I'll get you there. Go by the balcony and meet me in the back alley. I have to get my coat and purse and the bike. Be as quick as you can. Janna, you burn the evidence. Don't be too hasty about it; without the ladder they won't get here that quickly. There's kerosene in that can there and matches on the shelf. It's a good thing it's raining so hard, that will keep policemen away. Sef, I give you five minutes...I still have to get that bike out. 'Gird up now thy loins like a man and go and the Lord be with thee.' Don't say I didn't tell you we'd have bad luck, Janna."

As soon as Mina was gone, Sef took Janna in his arms and kissed her.

"My Janneke," he whispered. "If we both get out of this alive, I'll search for you the world over."

Janna could hardly breathe. "For me?" she asked incredulously. "Not for Nella?"

"No, for you." He gave her a mischievous smile. "I only hung up that picture to tease you...and because you look like her." He gave her one more kiss, and then the wardrobe swallowed him up. Janna stared after him, unable to think, trembling all over. But she had no time to brood. If she didn't destroy that evidence...

Feverishly she searched for incriminating scraps, adding them to the papers in the fireplace. She even found the yellow star! But when she tried to light the pile she found it wasn't easy. The paper caught fire, but smoldered around the edges, a red worm creeping from one blackened surface to another without appetite. Downstairs Janna heard people forcing the door and bursting into the chapel. She poked at the papers but only raised a halfhearted flame here and there that vanished as soon as she stopped. She began to panic. The evidence had to burn, it had to. Too much was at stake—the van Arkels' lives as well as Sef's and Mina's, not to speak of her parents'. Herr Rauter might not believe in their innocence!

Then she remembered the kerosene. She seized the can and poured the fuel on the papers. The flames leaped to meet it with a roar, the can exploded...but Janna had flung it away in time to save herself. The flames were raging on the floor now. Janna grabbed Sef's jug of drinking water and poured it on the flames, but that made them worse. The kerosene floated on the water and spread the fire all over the room, attacking all Sef's books and magazines. Thick black smoke was billowing up...the fire was uncontrollable. Janna ran for her life. The flames followed her, and so did the smoke. The whole room was a roaring furnace; black smoke poured through the wardrobe into Janna's bedroom. Janna ran down the stairs crying, "Fire! Fire!" The smoke pouring after her attracted more attention than her cries. People jostled and fought to get out of the house. Herr Oster, his face swollen and one eye closed, struggled to the phone and called the fire department.

"Our house has been struck by lightning," Janna heard him say. "Yes, it's burning..." The roar of devouring flames became louder and louder.

"Janna, Janna," cried Frau Oster.

"Here I am," shouted Janna, pushing through the mob.

"Otto!"

"Here I am!" Her father was carrying out wraps and umbrellas for the guests.

"Dietrich!" But there was no answer. The Baron was nowhere to be seen. The motley company fled into the street, into the pouring rain. By the flickering firelight they looked like a scene from an opera, only more bedraggled. The noise of people shouting and calling, the roaring of the flames, covered the sounds of the approaching fireboats. Neighbors on either side were also fleeing their houses. One of the old ladies stood by the canal, wringing her hands and crying, "My sister! My sister!" The other one seemed to be missing. People scurried about like ants. The firemen jumped ashore and roared through megaphones that everyone had to move to the other side of the canal.

"We need the space on this side," they shouted. Dutch policemen hustled people along. The old lady would not go.

"My sister is in there," she shrieked, pointing to the house. Tongues of flame were licking out of the windows. Mechtild was pushing and shoving to get nearer.

"Dietrich, Dietrich!" she cried.

Otto grabbed Janna's arm. "Mina. Have you seen Mina?"

"She went out the back way," said Janna. She was also looking for the Baron. And then she saw him, staggering out of the neighboring half-house, his face black with smoke, carrying the other old lady. She was alive; Janna could see her move and clutch at the Baron. He carried her to her sister, who cried, "Alida," and folded her in trembling arms. Neighbors immediately offered them shelter and they tottered off, supported by their friends. The Baron was wiping the soot from his face.

"Dietrich!" cried Mechtild. The Baron went to her. The heat was so intense by now that the last stragglers were running across the bridge, guarded by police. Janna and her father joined the crowd collecting on the other side of the canal, watching the spectacle. Even there they could feel the glow of the fire. Janna heard snatches of conversation.

"So disappointing. I thought it would at least be an arsenal, but it was only a gym. I wonder why they hid the door."

"Well, it wasn't pretty..."

"They must be insured for millions..."

"I said to Bruno, I said, pay up the premium, you never know, and I was right. This could have happened to us."

"I remember another curious case of lightning striking when I was in Wiesbaden..."

"What do you think of that marriage?"

"I always thought they were devoted, but it seems there was an affair going on all the time..."

Janna watched the powerful motors of the fireboats pump water from the canal through hoses onto the burning houses. The flames, mirrored in increasing brilliance in the water, spluttered when the spray hit them. Clouds of steam hissed up into the dark sky. The firemen gave up trying to save the burning houses and concentrated on the adjacent ones. The house which had shared the chimney in Sef's room was beginning to burn, but the firemen were able to control the flames. The house on the other side, where the children lived, was saved completely.

Janna could not keep her eyes from the glorious and awful spectacle. As she watched, tears dripped down her cheeks, mingling with the rain. She remembered the sleety day she had arrived, the comfortable dining room, her own room with its mysteries, the beautiful golden long room, the hidden altar...Oh, she hoped Sef and Mina were safe!

I've been Brunhilde all right, she thought. I really *have* lit a funeral pyre!

But no one suspected her. Everyone blamed the lightning. As Janna looked at the pulsing flames which twisted and reached for the sky, she remembered the paintings, especially the big one of the family...the rugs, the dollhouse...all, all gone. The light of the fire lit up the mournful group standing in the drizzle, scantily covered with wraps, holding umbrellas, unable to tear themselves away.

Janna saw the houses collapse in a shower of sparks. Built together, they perished together. As she watched the fire raging at a lower level, she realized that all traces of Sef and his work were now gone, erased more securely than by any other method she could have devised. She hoped that if the van Arkels knew, they'd forgive her.

Sef and Mina would read about the fire in the paper and have the sense to stay away. Mina would probably guess what had happened. She would probably stay with her brother now and keep house for him.

The glow faded and Janna felt forlorn. All she had learned to love these past months was being taken from her. Mina and Sef...would she ever see them again? Only her parents were left...or were they?

Janna saw her mother and the Baron standing close together under the shelter of a tree, deep in conversation. The Baron was pleading. Her mother looked as if she was crying. They would go off together, of course, like Siegmund and Sieglinde. That was what her father and the Baron had been fighting about. How could her mother do anything else? What would she do in her mother's place? The Baron was a hero...he was rich, handsome, owned a castle in Bavaria...How could that compare with her father, amiably distributing wraps and umbrellas? Janna's lips tightened.

"I won't have it," she muttered angrily. "I'll stop it..." But as she grabbed her ring, a feeling of shame overwhelmed her. What was she doing? With the flaming results of her last intervention before her eyes, she was ready to meddle again! She loved her mother, of course, and wanted to keep her...but what if her mother wanted to go? She was playing with forces she did not understand, with what the Baron called the wrong kind of power...tyranny and violence. Yes, because she was trying to force her mother—with what? With magic? Sef had said there was no magic; he'd said she was imagining it. But wasn't imagination itself a kind of magic? Hugo had said that thoughts could do harm.

The real trouble was that Janna didn't trust her mother. If she loved her mother enough, wouldn't she leave her free, as God had set Cain free? Even though it was risky, because people did such awful things when they were free! But Janna supposed it was the only way they could learn... hadn't her mother said that? Janna saw suddenly that she had been imagining magic to make things go the way she wanted, but it hadn't worked. She didn't like what had happened; everything had gone wrong. It was silly to think a girl like herself could guide events. She didn't have the power—and, what was more, she did not have the wisdom. Only God had that. Her mother was right to believe in God. It was much better than believing in a ring. Perhaps Brunhilde had seen that too, in the end ... Pulling the ring from her finger, Janna threw it into the canal. For a moment it winked in the afterglow of the fire; then it was gone. Janna would never play Brunhilde again. She would be just Janna, as Sef was just Sef.

The fireboats were still spraying water on the glowing ashes and blackened woodwork. Janna turned her head sadly. She was sure the Baron would now carry off her mother to his beautiful castle. That's where she belonged, her glamorous mother. She and her father would have to make the best of it. But how would they manage without a house, clothes, possessions? Janna realized suddenly that all she had to wear was her sopping wet Brunhilde costume...like those poor Jews... Only Janna wasn't going to a gas chamber.

And then someone brushed past her: the Baron in his swirling cloak. He looked tragic, defeated. Her mother stood alone by the canal, wrapped in the rain cloak Otto had found for her. Janna watched the Baron as he strode out of her life. She knew she would never see him again and her eyes filled with tears. She could have loved him so much!

"Mother!" cried Janna, flying into her arms. "Mother, are you going to stay with us?"

Her mother kissed her. "Darling," she said. "Is that what you've been worrying about? As if I could leave you! My goodness, what would you do without me, with no house to go to, no clothes to wear—and Papa sure to come down with bronchitis! Here, crawl under my cape, poor child, you're drenched..." Janna let herself be snuggled under her mother's open cloak.

"What will happen to us?" she sobbed. "Are you going to send me back to Erna?"

"Of course not," came her father's voice reassuringly from her other side, while a sheltering umbrella appeared above her. "I've already booked a hotel room and friends are lending us clothes. Am I glad I had my wallet with me and wasn't caught in fancy dress! No matter what happens, you'll stay with us. We won't do without her again, will we, Mechtild?"

"No, indeed," said Mechtild. "She wants to be an actress and she might as well start playing small parts. I did at her age. She can be a member of our company. She is really quite good, Otto, and we could use a child. We'll take her with us to Paris."

"To Paris? Do you mean it?" cried Otto joyfully.

"To Paris. I mean it."

The rain was still pouring down. The street was emptying as the spectators wandered off. The show was over. The houses had been reduced to ashes. The fireboats made ready to go.

But in Janna new hope flickered. She was going to act in real plays! She was going to be a member of her parents' company! She would stay with her parents, who were no longer ideal phantoms, existing only to make her happy, but real, imperfect people whom she had learned to love. They were a real family after all, for being a real family didn't mean playing games around a table: it meant sticking together through thick and thin, being loyal to each other. And someday, when all danger was over and the war a thing of the past, Janna would tell her parents the true story of the borrowed house.

The Place of *The Borrowed House* in Hilda van Stockum's Writing

In a letter, Hilda van Stockum offered the opinion that *The Borrowed House* was her best book. The truth of this assertion can be most fully appreciated in light of the ways in which *The Borrowed House*, first published in 1975 and thus representing her last published book, brings together the strengths of her earlier works in a concentrated fashion.

First, there is characterization. Perhaps the most striking aspect of Hilda's writing overall is the exuberance and life-like quality of her characters. Like Charles Dickens's, Hilda's brain seemed to be teeming with irrepressible personalities demanding to be let loose onto the page. Who could forget young Francis O'Sullivan of the Irish series—*The Cottage at Bantry Bay* (1938), *Francie on the Run* (1939), and *Pegeen* (1941)? Possessed of a lame foot, Francie never lets his infirmity become an obstacle to his adventures. When Doctor Casey chides him for walking the stairs of the hospital against his orders, for example, Francie protests, "'Deed then, I didn't...I slid down the banisters, so I did.'" As Hilda herself said, "Once one has a character like him the story more or less writes itself." Then there is...well, which of the Mitchell children shall we choose? They are all unforgettable. Responsible Joan, absent-minded Patsy, philosophical Peter, romantic Angela, inquisitive Timmy, and mischievous Catherine—each of the personalities in the Mitchell series (*The Mitchells: Five for Victory* [1945], *Canadian Summer* [1948], and *Friendly Gables* [1960]) has a vitality and integrity of his own. Hilda was as fertile as a creator of characters as she was as a mother (she had six children and eighteen grandchildren).

In *The Borrowed House,* Hilda has created another such memorable cast of characters. Mechtild, the mother, is glamorous and talented, but conflicted, and even ashamed of her faults. Mina, the cook, is rather pedantic in her constant quotation from Scripture, but she has such a big heart, and is so steadfast a refuge in time of trouble, that no one resents her for it. Even Heinz, the obnoxious boy upstairs, proves to have redeeming qualities of courage and loyalty, showing the veracity of what Edna St. Vincent Millay wrote in her foreword to *A Day on Skates*—that Hilda's children are "real children, not puppets." But the pièce de résistance is indeed the protagonist, Janna Oster. We see the story entirely from her perspective, and yet we are able to see her shortcomings, just as she is able ultimately to discover them as well. We feel for Janna when she has been slighted; for example, when her parents fail to listen to her stories when they are reunited after two years' separation. We are also moved to compassion when she becomes aware of how she has slighted others; when, for instance, she realizes with a jolt that she had no right to expect Sef to reveal to her that he is a Jew. And we rejoice when she overcomes her faults, such as when she admits she was wrong and apologizes to Sef. Here is a living, breathing girl whose sufferings we care about and whose growth we celebrate.

The second way in which *The Borrowed House* is a culmination of Hilda's work is in terms of plot. Hilda understood that a book was nothing without a story. She overflowed with stories. When she taught writing, she always emphasized, as Aristotle did, that character flowed out of the action, not the other way around. All of her twenty-two books (with the exception of *The Angels' Alphabet*, which is constructed on a different principle) centre on some important and interesting action which the reader aches to see resolved.

Here again, in *The Borrowed House*, Hilda has outdone herself. The plot of this novel concerns whether or not Janna and her parents will settle into a home safely. This plot is intricate in that it operates on numerous levels: Will Mechtild and Otto resolve their differences and overcome Mechtild's attraction to the Baron, allowing them to function as a true family? Will Janna successfully secure her parents' attention? More than that, however, will the foundation of the "home" prove solid—or is it based on oppression of others, in which case it is doomed to fall? The resolution of the plot is brilliant, in that it offers a resolution to all these threads. With the literal burning of the house, the Osters are free to leave behind the injustice of German occupation of Holland (symbolized by their displacement of the van Arkels) and make a new beginning; Mechtild is forced to decide between Otto and the Baron; and Janna finally receives the attention she craves from her parents as they incorporate her into their new world.

Finally, *The Borrowed House* can be seen as the summit of Hilda's expression of values in her writing. The family is central to her ethical vision, which is obvious in her novels based on large families teeming with life, such as the O'Sullivans and the Mitchells. In these novels of family life Hilda shows how we are all called to make way for others, to sacrifice some of our own desires for the good of others—family life would be impossibly difficult without this spirit. In *The Borrowed House*, however, family life is conspicuous mainly by its absence. For the first two chapters, Janna is separated from her family. And even after their reunion, Janna often feels a separation, whether because of her parents' busy lives or because of the gap she experiences between her (increasingly critical) view of what the Germans are doing, and theirs. But the relative fragility of the family in this novel serves not to undermine the importance of the family, but rather to underscore it. The family is the school in which we learn compassion, tolerance, and self-sacrifice. If we fail there, how can we expect to succeed elsewhere? Janna's growing acceptance of her parents as they really are is tied to her ability to accept others she has been taught to reject, such as Sef. In *The Borrowed House*, then, Hilda does not move away from family values but builds on them, showing that they are the foundation for a world in which, rather than trying to control others for our own gain, we accept and respect them as they are.

Christine Marlin Schintgen, July 2016

www.ingramcontent.com/pod-product-compliance
Lightning Source LLC
LaVergne TN
LVHW041935070526
838199LV00051BA/2801